Uncle Wiggily's Fortune

Howard Roger Garis

UNCLE WIGGILY'S
FORTUNE

BY
HOWARD R. GARIS
Author of "Sammie and Susie Littletail," "Johnnie and Billie
Bushytail," "Buddy and Brighteyes Pigg," "Joie,
Tommie and Kittie Kat," "Uncle Wiggily's
Travels," "Those Smith Boys," Series,
"The Island Boys," Series, etc.
ILLUSTRATED BY LOUIS WISA
R. F. FENNO & COMPANY
18 EAST SEVENTEENTH STREET
NEW YORK

CHILDREN'S BOOKS

By HOWARD R. GARIS

THE BEDTIME STORIES SERIES

EIGHT COLORED ILLUSTRATIONS

Price 75 cents each, postpaid

SAMMIE AND SUSIE LITTLETAIL

31 Rabbit Stories

JOHNNIE AND BILLIE BUSHYTAIL

31 Squirrel Stories

LULU, ALICE AND JIMMIE WIBBLEWOBBLE

31 Duck Stories

JACKIE AND PEETIE BOW WOW

31 Dog Stories

BUDDY AND BRIGHTEYES PIGG

31 Guinea Pig Stories

JOIE, TOMMIE AND KITTIE KAT

31 Cat Stories

CHARLIE AND ARABELLA CHICK

31 Chicken Stories

THE UNCLE WIGGILY SERIES

EIGHT COLORED ILLUSTRATIONS

Price 75 cents each, postpaid

UNCLE WIGGILY'S ADVENTURES

31 of the Old Gentleman Rabbit Stories

UNCLE WIGGILY'S TRAVELS

31 more of the Old Gentleman Rabbit Stories

UNCLE WIGGILY'S FORTUNE

31 other of the Old Gentleman Rabbit Stories

UNCLE WIGGILY'S AUTOMOBILE

31 different Old Gentleman Rabbit Stories

THOSE SMITH BOYS SERIES

FOUR ILLUSTRATIONS

Price 75 cents each, postpaid

THOSE SMITH BOYS

THOSE SMITH BOYS ON THE DIAMOND

THE ISLAND BOYS SERIES

FOUR ILLUSTRATIONS

Price 75 cents each, postpaid

THE ISLAND BOYS

(*Other volumes In preparation*)

STORY I
UNCLE WIGGILY AND THE FOX

Once upon a time, not so very many years ago, there lived an old gentleman rabbit named Uncle Wiggily Longears. He was a nice, quiet sort of a bunny, and he had lots of friends among other rabbits, and squirrels, and ducks, and doggies, and pussy cats, and mice and lambs, and all sorts of animals.

Most especially there was a muskrat lady, named Miss Jane Fuzzy-Wuzzy, who liked Uncle Wiggily very much. She made a crutch for him, when he had the rheumatism. She gnawed it out of a cornstalk for him, and painted it red, white and blue with raspberry jam.

Well, Uncle Wiggily was a funny old rabbit gentleman. He was always having adventures--which means things happening to you, such as stubbing your toe, or getting lost or things like that.

I have told you some of his adventures in a book before this one, and also about how he traveled all around looking for his fortune, so he would be rich. But he didn't find it for some time, though many things happened to him.

The last thing that happened, in the book before this one, was that he tore his nice coat, and a good tailor bird kindly mended it for him. And he stayed at her house for some time, bringing up coal, and sweeping the sidewalk, and things like that to be useful; for Uncle Wiggily was very kind.

He used to sleep in a hollow stump, near the nest of the tailor bird, and one night it rained so hard that he had to go to bed and pull the dried leaves up over him to keep warm. All night it rained, and in the morning Uncle Wiggily got up, and he was hoping it had cleared off, so he could travel on and seek his fortune, and get rich.

Out of bed hopped Uncle Wiggily. In one corner of the stump was his valise in which he carried his lunch and clean clothes and the like of that.

The day before, a bad wolf had chased Uncle Wiggily, catching him and tearing his coat, so that now the rabbit gentleman was quite stiff and sore. Still he managed to move about.

"Oh, dear me!" he exclaimed as he looked out of a hole in the stump, and saw the big rain drops still pattering down, "this is a very poor day for me to find my fortune. Still, I can't stay in on account of the weather, so I will get my breakfast and travel on."

He had some carrot and lettuce sandwiches in his valise and he ate these and then looked out to see if the rain had stopped, but it had not, I am sorry to say.

"Well," Uncle Wiggily said. "I don't like to get wet, but there is no help for it. I'll start out." Then he happened to think of something. "I know what I'll do!" he exclaimed. "I'll get the largest toadstool I can find, and use it for an umbrella."

Out he ran and soon he had picked a big toadstool that made as fine an umbrella as one could wish. Then, strapping his satchel to his back, where it would be out of the way, the old gentleman rabbit hopped off, holding the toadstool umbrella over his head, and limping along on his barber-pole crutch. And as he went over the meadows and through the woods he sang this little song, and sometimes when one sings it just at the right time, why it stops raining almost at once. But it has to be sung at the proper time. Anyhow this is the song:

"Splish-splash! Drip-dash!
How the raindrops fall!
When the weather gets too wet,
It isn't nice at all.
"Mr. Rain, oh, please go 'way!
For my feet are wet.
And you're splashing on my nose.
What? You can't stop yet?
"Won't you please be nice to me--
Make your raindrops dry.

I am sure you could do this
If you'd only try.
"Dry raindrops are very nice,
And if they would fall,
We could walk in showers, and
Not get wet at all."

Well, as soon as Uncle Wiggily had sung this song, he looked up quickly from under his toadstool umbrella to see if it had stopped raining, but it hadn't, and he got a drop right in his left eye, which made him sneeze so hard that his spectacles fell off. And they dropped right into a mud puddle.

"Ha, hum!" exclaimed the old gentleman rabbit, "this is a pretty kettle of fish!" Of course, he didn't mean that there was a kettle of fish in the mud puddle, but that was his manner of talking, because he was so surprised. "A very pretty kettle of fish, indeed!" cried the old gentleman rabbit, "and speaking of fish, I guess I'll have to fish for my spectacles."

So what did he do but use his red-white-and-blue-striped-barber-pole crutch for a fishing pole, and he dipped it down in the mud puddle and in a little while up came his glasses wiggling on the end of the crutch just like an eel.

"That is good luck!" said the rabbit, as he wiped off the mud and water and put on his spectacles, and he was just going to put his toadstool umbrella over his head again when he found out that the rain had stopped and he didn't need it.

Then he left the toadstool hanging on a berry bush by the mud puddle to dry, so that whoever came along next time would have an umbrella all ready for the rain.

"Well, now that the sun is coming out I must be on the watch for my fortune," said the old gentleman rabbit to himself. And he peered first on one side of the road and then on the other, but not a sign of his fortune could he see.

Then, all of a sudden he saw something shining golden yellow in a field close by.

"Ah, that must be a pile of yellow gold!" exclaimed Uncle Wiggily. "Now my fortune is made!" and he hopped over to the field. But alas! and alack-a-day! Instead of being gold the pile of yellow things were carrots.

"Well, it might be worse!" said the rabbit. "At least I can eat carrots. I wonder if whoever they belong to would mind if I took some?"

"I wouldn't mind a bit!" exclaimed a voice. "Take as many as you like, Uncle Wiggily," and up jumped Mr. Groundhog, who owned the carrots. "Take all you can eat and fill your valise," said Mr. Groundhog.

"Thank you very kindly," replied the rabbit, so he ate several carrots and filled his satchel with more, and then he and Mr. Groundhog talked about the weather, and things like that, until it was time for Uncle Wiggily to hop on again after his fortune.

But he didn't find it, and pretty soon it came on toward night, and the old gentleman rabbit looked for a place to stay while it was dark.

"I think this will do," he said, when he came to a small stone cave. "I'll just crawl in here with my carrots and my crutch," and in he crawled as nicely as a basket of shavings.

Pretty soon Uncle Wiggily was fast, fast asleep, and he never thought the least mite about any danger. But danger was close at hand just the same.

Hark! What's that creeping, creeping along under the bushes? Eh? What's that? Why, my goodness me sakes alive and a piece of pie! It's the fuzzy old fox! Yes, as true as I'm telling you, the old red fox had seen Uncle Wiggily go into the cave, and now he was snooping and snipping up to catch him if he could.

"Oh, I'll soon have a fine time!" said the fox in a whisper, smacking his lips. Into the cave he crawled, and in the darkness he happened to knock over Uncle Wiggily's crutch, which was standing in a corner. Quickly the old gentleman rabbit awakened when he heard the noise. Up he jumped and he cried out:

"Who's there?"

"I'm the fox," was the answer, "and I came to catch you."

But do you s'pose Uncle Wiggily was afraid? Not a bit of it. He ran to his valise and he took out a pawful of carrots with their sharp points, and before that fox could even sneeze the rabbit threw one carrot at him and hit him on the nose, for Uncle Wiggily could see in the dark.

Then he threw another carrot and hit the fox on the ear, and then he threw still another one and he hit him on the two eyes, and that fox was so frightened and surprised that he jumped out of the second-story window of the cave house and sprained his toenail. Then he ran back to his den and didn't bother Uncle Wiggily any more that night, and the rabbit slept in peace and quietness, and dreamed about Santa Claus and ice-cream popcorn balls.

But Uncle Wiggily had another adventure next day. I'll tell you about it in a little while, when, in case some one sends me a mud pie with a cherry on the top, the story will be about Uncle Wiggily and the bird's nest.

STORY II
UNCLE WIGGILY AND THE BIRD'S NEST

"Now, I must be very careful to-day," said Uncle Wiggily to himself as he got up after sleeping in the stone cave, as I told you he did in the story before this one. "I must be very careful so that fox won't catch me."

So, very carefully and cautiously, he crept to the window of the stone cave house, and looked down, but the red fox was not there. The sun was brightly shining and the old gentleman rabbit could see the big dent made in the soft ground, where the fox had landed when he jumped out of the window and sprained his toenail.

"My! that certainly was a narrow escape for me," thought Uncle Wiggily. Then he fried some of Mr. Groundhog's carrots for his breakfast and, putting some of them in his valise for his lunch, off he started once more to seek his fortune.

He hadn't gone very far before he came to a place where he heard a funny buzzing sound. It was just like a small saw-mill away off in the woods, where the men saw logs into boards in order that houses may be built.

"Oh, my suz dud and a piece of red paper!" exclaimed Uncle Wiggily. "I must be careful or I might get my nose cut off in that saw-mill." So he was very careful, and, after he had listened a while longer, he wasn't quite so sure that it was a saw-mill that he heard, for he could hear a little voice crying:

"Oh, dear. I'll never get loose! I'm caught fast! Oh, if some one would only help me!"

"Ha! That is some one in trouble!" said the rabbit. "I'm going to see if I can't help them." So he bravely kept on through the woods, and the buzzing sound became louder, until, all at once, the old gentleman rabbit saw a nice, good bumble bee caught in the web of a big, black spider.

The bee was all tangled up in the web, and it was his wings fluttering to and fro and up and down that made the buzzing sound.

"Ha! Can't you get loose?" asked the rabbit.

"Indeed he can't!" cried the big, black spider lady, as she sat all hunched up in a corner of her web, waiting for the bee to get more tangled up and all tired out, so she could bite him. "He'll never get away from me," said the spider lady, sassy-like.

"Oh, ho! We will have to see about that!" exclaimed the rabbit. "I am afraid you are mistaken, Mrs. Spider. I am very sorry to have to spoil your cobweb, but I must help my friend, the bumble bee." And with that Uncle Wiggily took his crutch, and broke the web away from the bee's legs and wings so that he was loose and could fly away.

"I never can thank you enough, Uncle Wiggily," said the bee to the rabbit, "and if ever I can do you, or any of your friends, a favor I will. Don't forget to call on me."

"And if ever I can bite you, I will, Mr. Rabbit," said the spider in her crossest voice, as she set to work to mend her cobweb net so that she might catch some one else. Oh! but she was angry, though perhaps we can't blame her.

Well, Uncle Wiggily didn't worry much about what the spider said, as he knew he was going to travel on for a long distance after his fortune, and he didn't think she would come after him, and she didn't.

On and on hopped the old gentleman rabbit, sometimes going slowly and sometimes fast, and once in a while he would go up a hill, and then, again, he would go down. And so it went on. When it wasn't one thing it was another. But he didn't find his fortune anywhere.

Pretty soon, when it was nearly noon, Uncle Wiggily began to feel hungry, so he looked for a nice place where he might sit down and eat his lunch. He saw a shady tree, and he walked toward that, and, just as he did so, he happened to look up, and there, hanging from a branch, was a sort of brown-colored round object, that looked like a small bag.

"Ha! I think I know what that is!" exclaimed Uncle Wiggily. "That is the nest of a stingery hornet, and if I go too close I'll get stung. I'll just keep away, and go somewhere else to eat my lunch."

Uncle Wiggily started off, but at that moment he heard some voices calling. And this is what they said:

"Oh, dear! How hungry we are! Oh, when will mamma come back! Oh, if we only had something to eat!"

"Hum! I hope those hornets don't see me, and come out to bite me," said the rabbit.

And, would you ever believe it? the next moment those who had been calling must have seen Uncle Wiggily, for a voice exclaimed:

"Oh, good Mr. Rabbit won't you please come here? We can't get out, and our mamma has gone to the store for something to eat, and she hasn't come back; and we're so hungry. Please help us!"

"No indeed, I will not!" said Uncle Wiggily firmly. "I don't want to be unkind," he said, "but I am afraid you will sting me, you little hornets!"

"Why, the idea!" cried all the voices at once. "We are not hornets, we are only little birdies, and this is a bird's nest."

"Why, bless my whiskers!" exclaimed Uncle Wiggily. "I believe I have made a mistake." Then he put on his glasses, and surely enough he saw that the brown object like a bag was a nest, and it was full of little birds who could not yet fly very much, for their wings were not strong enough.

"Now, will you help us?" the birdies asked the rabbit. "Help us, please do; for we won't hurt you!"

"Bless my whiskers! Of course I will!" Uncle Wiggily cried, and he at once opened his valise and gave them all they could eat.

"Now I will go look for your mamma," he said. Off he started, but he had not gone very far before he heard the birdies in the nest crying:

"Help! Help! Help!" Uncle Wiggily looked back, and there was a great, big, ugly snake crawling up the tree to get the little birds.

"Oh, I must stop that!" exclaimed the rabbit, and back he started to hop to the nest. But he was quite a distance off, and he saw that he could not get back in time to drive off the snake. "Oh, what shall I do?" he cried. "If only the bumble bee would come along now and sting that snake the crawly creature would run away!"

And, would you ever believe it if I didn't tell you? At that moment along buzzed the bee and he saw the snake and stung him so that the snake was glad to jump away, and not hurt the little birdies. Then Uncle Wiggily and the little birds thanked the bee, who buzzed off to find some apple blossom honey. And pretty soon the mamma bird came home from the store, and she was very grateful to the rabbit for taking care of her little ones.

The reason she was away so long was because a boy threw a stone at her and made her spill the bread she had for her birdies. So she had to go back to the store for more.

"If you stay with us for a few days we will help you look for your fortune," said the mamma bird, and Uncle Wiggily did stay, and he had an adventure.

I'll tell you about it on the next page, when, in case the popcorn ball doesn't roll off the table and bump the kittie's nose, the story will be about Uncle Wiggily and a big rat.

STORY III
UNCLE WIGGILY AND A BIG RAT

When Uncle Wiggily had fed the little birds in the nest, after he and the bumble bee had saved them from the snake, as I told you in another story, the mamma bird said she could not do enough for the old gentleman rabbit.

"I will have my little ones sing a song for you," she went on. "Come now, birdies, sing for Uncle Wiggily."

So this is the song the little birds in the nest sang:

"Uncle Wiggily is good,
Uncle Wiggily is kind,
And we hope with all our hearts,
That his fortune he may find.
"Gold and silver, diamonds, too,
Ice-cream cones and candy sticks,
And we hope that he can buy,
Two red monkeys who do tricks."

"Oh! that is a very nice song, birdies," said the rabbit, as he took off his hat and made a low bow. "But," he went on, "I don't know as I care for red monkeys who do tricks. What in the world would I do with them?"

"Why, you could give them to us and they would amuse us when our mamma was away," said a little bird who had some feathers sticking crossways in her tail.

"Yes, I suppose I could give you the monkeys," went on the old gentleman rabbit, "but I hardly expect to find any in my travels-- especially red ones."

"Won't you stay to supper with us?" asked the mamma bird, "and we would also be pleased to have you stay all night. Oh, no!" she suddenly exclaimed. "I don't see how you can stay all night."

"I can if you want me to," said Uncle Wiggily, for he thought perhaps the bird was afraid the snake might come back in the darkness, and the old gentleman rabbit made up his mind that if the crawly creature did sneak up, he would hit it with his crutch.

"Well, of course we'd like to have you stay," said the mamma bird, slowly, "but the truth of the matter is that I have no place for you to sleep. You see, our nest is so small; and besides, I never knew of a rabbit in a nest, except at Easter time."

"Of course," agreed Uncle Wiggily, "I never thought of that. However, it is very kind of you, and I'll travel on until I find a hollow stump, or some place like that where I can sleep."

"Oh, mamma!" exclaimed a little boy birdie, "why can't Uncle Wiggily make a tent, and sleep in it right near our nest? He can pretend that he is camping out."

"The very thing!" cried the rabbit. "I'll do it. But of what can I make a tent?"

"We can give you the sticks and the cloth," said the mamma bird, so she showed Uncle Wiggily where there were some nice long sticks, like fishing poles, and some old sheets from a bed that no one wanted.

"That will make a fine tent!" said Uncle Wiggily, "and I'm sure I will sleep in it very nicely."

So he set to work to make the tent. First he stuck one stick in the ground, and then he stuck another stick in, and then still another, until he had about seven sticks sticking around in a circle. Next the mamma bird pulled them together at the top, just like the Indians' tents in the Wild West show, and then she and all the other little birdies tied them with blades of grass for strings, and helped put the cloth around to cover up the sticks.

Then, if you'll believe me, and I hope you do, there was the tent, pointed on top and round at the bottom, just like those chocolate drops with white cream inside that are so nice and soft.

"Ha! this is a very fine tent indeed!" exclaimed Uncle Wiggily. "Now I'll move my valise and crutch inside, and I'll feel right at home."

"And we'll help you make your bed," said the little birds, and away some of the strongest of them flew around, gathering up in their bills dozens of soft leaves, and soon they had made as fine a bed, almost, as baby's crib.

Then supper was ready. And now, let me see, what did they have for supper? Oh, I know! There was some rose leaf pie, and some violets with sugar on, and some bird seed boiled in molasses, and for Uncle Wiggily there was the loveliest turnip cake, with carrot frosting on top, that you have ever seen. Oh! it was most delicious, and it makes me hungry even to typewrite about it, and I'm sure you would like it if you had some.

"Now it's bedtime for you birdies," said the mamma, and she sang them a little lullaby and soon their eyes were tightly shut.

"Yes, and I guess I had better get in my tent," said the rabbit, so in he crawled beneath the cloth that was stretched over the poles, down upon the bed of leaves he lay, and soon he too was fast, fast asleep.

Well, along about in the middle of the night Uncle Wiggily was awakened by hearing something scratching on the side of the tent.

"Ha, hum! I wonder what that can be?" he asked. "Perhaps it is the bad snake coming back. If it is I must get ready with my crutch."

So he reached out in the darkness to get hold of the crutch and just then he saw a light flickering. And a moment later something big and black, with long whiskers, and long sharp teeth, came right inside the tent. And Uncle Wiggily saw that it was a big rat, and that rat had a bottle, and in it were a lot of flickering lightning bugs, and that was the lantern the rat carried, so that he could see in the dark.

"Oh, hello! So you're in here, eh?" asked the rat as he waved his whiskers to and fro at Uncle Wiggily. "Well, I'm disappointed."

"Why so?" asked the rabbit, as he got his crutch and stood ready to hit the rat in case he sprang forward to use his sharp teeth. "Why are you disappointed?"

"Because I thought the birds were in here," said the rat. "I mean to take them all off to my den and make them sing me to sleep. But since you are here, I'll begin on you first, and then I'll go out and pull down the birds' nest."

"Oh, no, you can't do that," said Uncle Wiggily firmly.

"Why not?" asked the rat, surprised-like. "Who will stop me?"

"I will!" bravely cried Uncle Wiggily, and with that he raised his crutch, and he tickled that rat right on the end of his long tail. And the rat was so surprised that he thought he had been struck by a policeman's club. So he jumped around, and, as he did so, Uncle Wiggily threw a piece of cherry pie at him, and it was all soft and squashy like, and the juice ran down in the rat's eyes, and so blinded him that he couldn't see to bite the rabbit, or even a piece of cheese.

"Now, you get right out of this tent, and don't you dare to harm the birds!" cried the old gentleman rabbit, and that rat went right out, taking his long thin tail with him, but forgetting his lightning bug lantern, which he left on the ground.

So Uncle Wiggily looked out to make sure that the rat didn't go near the birds' nest and the bad creature didn't, but he scurried back to his hole in the rocks, feeling quite savage-like and more disappointed than ever.

Next the rabbit took the cork out of the rat's bottle-lantern and he let the poor lightning bugs go, and they were very thankful. And then the rabbit stretched out on the leaves again, and went to sleep until morning and nothing more disturbed him.

Now if the knives and forks don't jump up and down on the table, and upset the sugar bowl, so that it scares the vinegar bottle, I'll tell you next about Uncle Wiggily on a raft.

Uncle Wiggily and the Big River Rat

STORY IV
UNCLE WIGGILY ON A RAFT

"Well, I think I will be traveling along now," said Uncle Wiggily to the bird family the next morning after he had had the adventure with the rat. "I must have another try at finding my fortune. And, perhaps, since you sang such a nice song for me yesterday, you little birds will sing another as I am leaving."

"Of course they will," said their mamma, so she gave a few trills and chords to start them off, and the birdies sang this:

"Dear old Uncle Wiggily,
We wish that you could stay
And live near our nest always,
To drive the rats away.
"But if you now must leave us,
Then we will wish for you,
That you may have much happiness
Whatever you may do."

"I'm sure that's very nice," said the rabbit, "and now I'll bid you good-bye and travel on."

"But you must take some lunch with you," said the mamma bird, and she gave him some more cherry pie to make up for the piece he had thrown at the rat.

Uncle Wiggily went on and on, and pretty soon he came to a place in the woods where there was a tall tree. And some distance up from the ground there was a hole in this tree trunk.

"Ha, hum!" exclaimed Uncle Wiggily, "perhaps there may be gold in that tree hole. Now if I could only climb up to see, I might find my fortune."

Well, you know how it is with rabbits. They can't climb a tree even as well as a girl can, and, of course, Uncle Wiggily had to remain on the ground.

"If only Johnnie or Billie Bushytail were here now," thought the rabbit, "those squirrel boys could climb the tree for me. But I know what I'll do, I'll tie a stone to a string, and I'll put some molasses on the stone and throw it up into the hole in the tree. Then, if there is any gold there, it may stick to the molasses on the stone, and I can pull some down."

So he did this, and he made the string fast to the stone, and was all ready to throw it up when he happened to remember that he had no molasses.

"How careless of me! What shall I do?" he exclaimed. And a voice answered:

"I will give you some molasses, Uncle Wiggily."

The old gentleman rabbit looked around, and there was a nice, green grasshopper, and, as she had some molasses with her, she put quite a lot on the stone. Then the rabbit threw it up at the hole in the tree, but a most surprising thing happened.

For, instead of being gold in the hole there were two unpleasant old owls there, and when the molasses-covered stone popped in on them it awakened them from their sleep, for owls sleep in the day time, and fly about at night, you know.

"Who threw that stone?" cried one owl.

"I don't know," answered the other owl, and she gnashed her sharp beak, "but whoever it was I'm going to bite him!"

"Oh, run! Run for your life, Uncle Wiggily!" cried the grasshopper, as the two owls stuck their heads out of the hole in the tree. "Hop away!"

So Uncle Wiggily hopped off, and the grasshopper hopped also, and the two owls flopped down after them. But the savage birds could not see very well in the day time, and one went ker-bunk into a tree, and the other went ker-thump into a briar bush, and they were all tangled up, and so Uncle Wiggily and the grasshopper got safely away.

16

"Well, I didn't get any fortune that time," said the rabbit sorrowfully as he hopped down a hill. "But perhaps I may find it soon."

The next place he came to was a big river, and, as he stood on the bank and looked across, it seemed to Uncle Wiggily that he could see a big field of gold on the other side.

"I must get over there," he said to himself, "and I am sure I will find my fortune. But how am I going to do it? That river is too wide for me to jump across, and it is too wide for me to swim. If I only had a boat I would be all right."

The old gentleman rabbit looked around for a boat, but none was at hand. Then he happened to think of something that Sammie and Susie Littletail once did.

"That's what I'll do!" exclaimed Uncle Wiggily, "I'll make a raft." So he got some planks and boards and sticks, and he laid them crossways one upon the other, and tied them together with strong pieces of wild grape vine. Then he had a raft on which he could sit and push himself across the river, almost as well as if he had a rowboat.

"Now, I'll put my valise on board, and hop on myself, and away we'll go!" he cried, and he was very much pleased with the raft that he had made. Into the water he shoved it, and in the middle of the raft he placed his valise. Then he got on, and shoved off, using his crutch for a pushing pole.

Out into the middle of the river went Uncle Wiggily on the raft, and he was having a fine sail. Then all at once he felt hungry, so he stopped pushing the raft, opened his valise and took out a piece of cherry pie.

Well, as true as I'm telling you, just as he was eating it he heard a swirling noise in the water behind him and a savage voice cried out:

"Ha! Now I have you! Give me that piece of cherry pie or I'll upset the raft and you'll get all wet!"

Uncle Wiggily looked around, and there, swimming right up to him was a big, snicky-snooky water rat--a second cousin to the rat that got into Uncle Wiggily's tent the night before.

"Give me that pie!" cried the rat, as she put her claws on the raft. "Give it to me."

"No, indeed, I will not," replied Uncle Wiggily, as politely as one can speak to a rat.

Then the bad creature tried to climb up on the raft, but the rabbit took his crutch and put it down in the water and pushed along on the bottom of the river, sending the raft along very swiftly.

"Oh, I'll get you yet!" cried the rat, as she swam on after the raft. Faster and faster she swam, and faster and faster did Uncle Wiggily push, until he was all tired out, and he felt sure he would be caught and carried away by the bad rat. And then a voice in the air overhead suddenly cried out:

"Take your handkerchief, Uncle Wiggily, and make a sail out of it. Then the wind will blow you along so fast that the rat can't catch you. Make a sail!"

And Uncle Wiggily did so. He stuck the crutch up for a mast on the raft, and then he fastened his largest red handkerchief to the crutch. And the wind caught it, and blew upon that red handkerchief sail and the raft skimmered over the river so fast that the bad rat was left far, far behind, and so couldn't catch the rabbit.

It was the kind mamma bird who had called to the rabbit gentleman to tell him what to do.

And in a little while Uncle Wiggily was safe on the other shore and he hopped off the raft and ran toward the field that looked as if it was filled with gold.

Whether he found any or not, and what happened to him, I'll tell you on the next page, when the story will be about Uncle Wiggily in a boat--that is if our puppy dog doesn't sit down in the fly-paper and get so stuck up so he can't gnaw a bone when he goes to the kitten's party.

STORY V
UNCLE WIGGILY IN A BOAT

When Uncle Wiggily got to the edge of the yellow golden-colored field after jumping off the raft, as I told you in the story before this one, the old gentleman rabbit rubbed his eyes, and then rubbed them again, for he wasn't quite sure of what he saw.

"Why!" he exclaimed, as he put on his spectacles in order to see better. "I have made quite a mistake. This isn't a field of gold at all, it is only a field of golden rod, which is a flower."

"Ah, if it is golden rod, perhaps if you wait long enough it will turn into chunks of gold," said a little voice down on the ground, and, glancing there, Uncle Wiggily saw a little ant with a tiny loaf of bread on her back. "Why don't you wait for that to happen, Mr. Rabbit?" she asked.

"Oh, it would never happen," said Uncle Wiggily. "This golden rod is a flower, and it will always remain a flower. I am disappointed once more about finding my fortune. I thought when I saw this shining yellow color from my raft, after I got away from the rat, that I had found the gold for which I am looking. But, never mind, this flower is very pretty," and he picked a bunch of it and smelled of it.

And some of the yellow dust of the posy-blossom got up the rabbit's twinkling nose, and he sneezed so hard that his glasses fell off. But the ant kindly picked them up for the old gentleman though he had to reach over to take them from her, as she was so small that she hardly came up to the rabbit's knee.

"Well, I must get home to my little ones," said the ant with a loaf of bread. "I hope you have good luck, Uncle Wiggily."

"Thank you very kindly," spoke the rabbit, and then he put a golden rod flower in his button-hole and hopped on to look for his fortune.

Pretty soon, not so very long, in a little while, the rabbit came to a nice smooth rock which was long and slanting, just like a hill down which you slide on your sleds in the winter time. Only, of course, there was no snow or ice now, as it was summer.

"Ha! Now if I was a little younger, and didn't have the rheumatism, I'd slide down that rock!" exclaimed the rabbit. "I wish Sammie and Susie Littletail were here, for they would enjoy this very much. And so would Johnnie and Billie Bushytail, the squirrel brothers, not to mention the puppy dogs."

Then the rabbit looked at the nice, smooth rocky slide, and all of a sudden he heard a voice singing:

"Lumps of pudding and pieces of pie
My mamma gave me when I was a boy,
And for those things I used to cry--
For lumps of pudding and pieces of pie!"

"Hum! I wonder who that can be?" asked Uncle Wiggily, and then he heard some one laugh and shout, and a great big boy, about as big as two barrels of molasses, burst out of the bushes.

"Why, it's the giant's little boy!" exclaimed Uncle Wiggily in great surprise.

"Yes, that's who I am!" cried the boy who was as large as two barrels of molasses, and a can of condensed milk besides. "How are you, Uncle Wiggily? Have you found your fortune yet?"

"No," said the rabbit a bit sadly, "I have not."

"Never mind," spoke the giant's little boy, "come on and have a slide, it's lots of fun," and with that the big boy threw himself down on the smooth rock, just as if he were on a sled, and away he whizzed down the hill as nicely as a cake of soft soap slips into the bathtub.

"I believe I will try it!" exclaimed the old rabbit gentleman, so, taking a firm hold of his crutch and valise he sat down on the smooth rock, and away he whizzed down after the boy who was as big as two barrels of sweet molasses and an ice-cream cone also.

21

Faster and faster went the rabbit, and faster and faster went the giant's little boy, until, all of a sudden, the boy slipped off the stone and landed in a big pile of hay, and wasn't hurt at all.

"I wonder if that's what will happen to me?" thought Uncle Wiggily, and he was just looking to see where he would land, and he was hoping it would be in a feather bed, when, as quickly as you can catch an alligator, if ever there's one to catch, the old gentleman rabbit slid off the rock, and down he came, plump on top of a big toadstool, and he wasn't hurt a bit; only sort of jounced up and down like.

"My! That was a fine slide," he said. Then he looked up and he saw that he was right on the shore of a little lake, and close at hand was a rowboat with oars in, and on the boat was a sign which read:

"PLEASE TAKE A RIDE IN ME ON
THE LAKE."

"Ha! That is very polite of some one," said the rabbit. "I believe I will take a ride in the boat. And perhaps I may find my fortune in it."

Then he looked more carefully, and he saw that there was a box in the boat, and on the box was a sign which read:

"PLEASE DO NOT OPEN THIS
BOX."

"Hum! Perhaps there is gold in there. But I won't open it to see until some one tells me I may," thought the rabbit.

So he got into the boat, and he stuck the oars through the oarlocks, which are places made for them, then he dipped the wide part of the oar into the water and pulled on the handle part and, my land sakes, flopsy-dub! Uncle Wiggily was rowing as nicely as you please.

Well, he rowed on and on, until he was out in the middle of the lake, and then, all of a sudden, he heard a funny noise inside the box. It was a sort of scratching, growling noise, and before the rabbit could do anything, the top of the box flew open and out stepped a little black bear. Oh, but Uncle Wiggily was frightened!

"Ah, ha! Now I have you, just where I want you, Mr. Rabbit," said the bear. "This is the last of you. Burr-r-r-r!"

Well, Uncle Wiggily was so frightened that he didn't know what to do, for he surely thought his end had come. Then he happened to remember that he had some cherry pie in his valise, and he knew that bears are very fond of sweet stuff.

"I know what I'll do," thought the rabbit. "I'll give the bear some pie, and when he isn't looking I'll row toward shore, and perhaps I can get away from him." So he quickly opened his satchel, took out the pie and gave it to the bear most politely.

"Ha! this is very good," said the bear in a grillery, growlery voice, as he took the pie. "I will eat this first and afterward I'll attend to your case!"

And when the bear was eating the pie, and licking the sweet, red juice off his clawy paws, Uncle Wiggily rowed toward shore. But he wasn't yet quite near enough to jump out of the boat, so he gave the bear another piece of pie and rowed a little closer to shore.

The bear was so interested in eating the cherries from the pie, and sucking the juice off his paws, that he never noticed what was going on. But finally he glanced up, and when he saw how near the shore the rabbit had rowed the boat the bear cried:

"Ah! ha! So that's your trick, eh? Well, I'll scratch you, anyhow."

And with that he made a spring for the rabbit, but Uncle Wiggily was too quick for him. Grabbing up his crutch and valise, the rabbit jumped out of the boat and landed on shore, and then the wind suddenly sprang up and blew the boat and bear in it out into the middle of the lake, and Uncle Wiggily was safe, I'm glad to say, for the bear couldn't swim to shore that day on account of having no bathing suit.

Then, hopping on, Uncle Wiggily looked all over for his fortune. But he did not find it right away. And he had another adventure soon. What it was I'll tell you almost immediately, which is very soon, when in case the pink cow doesn't eat the chocolate pudding from off the back stoop where the cook sets it to cool, the next story will be about Uncle Wiggily at the seashore.

STORY VI
UNCLE WIGGILY AT THE SEASHORE

One morning Uncle Wiggily was hopping along a dusty road. It was the day after he had gotten away from the bad black bear in the boat, and the old gentleman rabbit was thinking of what great danger he had been in.

"I must certainly be more careful," he thought, "and not get in every boat I see. Why, just think of it! If that bear had eaten me up I couldn't search for my fortune any more," and this so frightened Uncle Wiggily that he looked all around and behind the bushes, fearing the bear might, after all, have come ashore and be chasing after him.

But no bear was there, for he had fallen out of the boat and caught cold and had gone to bed, after drinking some hot honey lemonade. The old gentleman rabbit felt better, when he saw there was no bear, but it was so hot that he was thirsty, so he looked for a place to get a drink. Pretty soon he saw a nice, cold spring, and he took three drinks of water and part of another one.

And just as the rabbit was drinking the last drop of water he heard a funny noise out in the road, and, looking up, he saw a whole lot of children going past. Some of them were barefooted, and some had little tin pails and shovels in their hands, and some had red balloons and some blue or green ones. Some of the children had on bathing suits and a few had their little dresses tucked up as far as they could go, and they were dancing along on their slim white legs, as happy as happy could be.

"Why, this certainly is very strange," thought the rabbit. "I wonder where they can all be going? Perhaps it is to a circus parade. I must go see, for I might meet my friend the elephant there. Oh, this will be some fun! Is it a circus parade?" he called aloud.

"No, it isn't a circus parade," said a voice at Uncle Wiggily's side, and, looking down, the old gentleman rabbit saw the kind grasshopper who had once given him some molasses.

"If it isn't a circus parade, what is it?" asked the rabbit.

"These children are going to the seashore to bathe and paddle in the salty ocean waves," went on the grasshopper, "and some of them will build sand houses, or dig wells for the water to fill up. Why don't you go, Uncle Wiggily? Perhaps you may find your fortune there."

"I believe I will," said the rabbit. "Won't you come along?" Well, the grasshopper said he would, so off they hopped together, the hoppergrass--I beg your pardon,--I mean the grasshopper--and the rabbit.

Pretty soon they heard the noise of the waves pounding on the sandy shores, and they could smell the salt breeze and it made them hungry for clam chowder and lobsters and crabs and things like that. Then they saw ever so many more children running along and in a little while they were at the seashore.

"Well, now to look for my fortune," said the rabbit, as he watched the waves rush up on the sand with a big noise and lots of foam, and then they would tumble out to the sea again. "How do you think I had better go about it, Mr. Grasshopper?"

"If I were you I would dig in the sand," said the grasshopper. "Sometimes men, who were called pirates, used to bury gold in the sand, and perhaps there is some of their money left. You dig and I will watch you."

"But I have nothing with which to dig," said the rabbit.

"Oh, you may take my shovel," said a little girl with her dress tucked up high so that it would not get wet. "I am going in wading, so I won't need it."

"Thank you kindly," said the rabbit gentleman to the little girl, and then she went in wading, and a wave splashed up all over her, no matter if her dress was above her knees, and her mamma called to her to be more careful, and not to get so wet.

So Uncle Wiggily began to dig. Deeper and deeper he dug in the sand, while the grasshopper watched him. And every few minutes Uncle Wiggily would look down the hole to see if there was any gold among the grains of sand, but there wasn't any.

All around were children having lots of fun. One boy made a tunnel, and then he played that some sticks of wood were steam cars and he pushed them through the tunnel and puffed out his cheeks to pretend it was the engine choo-chooing.

And a little girl made a garden in the sand, with seaweed for flowers and clam-shells for a house, and she and another little girl had a play-party. Oh, it was great fun!

Then a big boy stretched out on the sand, and another boy covered him all up, from the tips of his toes to the tips of his nose, and he left his nose out so the boy could breathe. Well, the grasshopper and Uncle Wiggily looked at all this fun going on and they were happy as they could be. And the rabbit kept on digging the hole down in the sand, hoping he would soon come to the gold.

And then all of a sudden, before you could count up to forty-'leven, the hole which Uncle Wiggily was digging filled up with water, just like a well.

"Oh, my!" exclaimed the rabbit. "This is certainly bad luck. Now I can't find any gold. What am I to do?"

"I guess you'll have to dig another hole," said the grasshopper. "But perhaps there is gold at the bottom of this one, after all. Let's get a pail and dip out the water, then we may see the gold."

So the little girl who had loaned the rabbit her shovel let Uncle Wiggily take her pail to dip out the water. But the funny part of it was that the faster he dipped out the water the more came in, until there was enough for two wells. Then even the grasshopper helped dip out the water with another little pail, but it did no good.

The rabbit and the grasshopper were both so interested in what they were doing that they didn't notice a big crab crawling up behind them, and the first thing they knew Uncle Wiggily felt some one pinch him on his little short tail.

"Ha! What is that?" he cried, turning around quickly, and then he saw the crab, with its big blue claws pinching him.

"Ouch! Oh, my!" cried the rabbit. "Whatever shall I do?"

"I'll help pull him off!" shouted the grasshopper, but he was not strong enough, and the crawly crab still clung to the rabbit's tail.

"Why are you pinching me?" asked the rabbit, as he tried to reach around and pull off the crab, only he found he could not do it.

"I am pinching you because you dug a hole down in my sandy beach," said the crab, "and I'm going to hold on to you until you give me a thousand pieces of cheese for my supper."

"Oh, I can never get that many!" cried the rabbit. "Will no one help me get away from this crab?" But all the children had run home to dinner and there was no one to help the rabbit, until all of a sudden, a big wave washed up, and almost covered Uncle Wiggily.

He could just manage to breathe, and he sprang up on the beach to get beyond the water, and the grasshopper hopped out of the way also. But the wave was a good one after all, for as soon as the crab felt the water sloshing up around him he let go of the rabbit's tail to swim away, and that's how Uncle Wiggily was saved from the crab, even if he didn't find any gold, and he was very glad his tail wasn't pinched off.

The old gentleman rabbit remained at the seashore for several days, and he had many adventures. And, in case I find a peanut shell with a red popcorn ball inside of it, the next bedtime story will be about Uncle Wiggily and the big lobster.

STORY VII
UNCLE WIGGILY AND THE LOBSTER

"Where are you going to stay to-night, Uncle Wiggily?" asked the grasshopper of the old gentleman rabbit, after the wave had rolled up and washed away the crab that had hold of the bunny's tail, I told you about last, you remember. "Are you going to stay at the seashore?" asked the grasshopper, as he looked at his left hind leg and blinked his two eyes, sort of thoughtful-like.

"Oh, yes, I like it here very much," said Uncle Wiggily, "and I'm going to stay, but as true as I live I don't know where I can sleep to-night."

"Couldn't you build a sand house, such as we see the children making?" asked the grasshopper.

"Oh, no, for in the night it might fall down on me, and the sand would get in my ears. Or a big wave might roll up on the shore and wash me out to sea. Oh, dear, isn't it a puzzle what to do when you are seeking your fortune?"

"Oh, don't feel so badly over it," begged the grasshopper. "We will look around and see what we can find."

"Where are you going to stay, Mr. Grasshopper?" asked the rabbit.

"Who, me? Oh, I am going to crawl under a leaf and sing myself to sleep as I always do; but for you, a leaf is hardly large enough."

"Not unless it was a palm-leaf fan," spoke the old gentleman rabbit. "But come on, we will look around."

So they hopped up and down the beach where the ocean waves were rolling along with a booming noise. All the children had gone in by this time, as it was getting dark and rather lonesome. Uncle Wiggily and the grasshopper looked, and they looked, and they looked still more, but they could find no place for the rabbit to stay. At last the old gentleman rabbit said:

"Well, Mr. Grasshopper, you had better get along and look for the leaf under which you are going to sleep, or else it will get so dark that you can't find your way."

"But what will you do, Uncle Wiggily? I don't like to leave you all alone."

"Oh, if it comes to the worst I can sleep out here on the sands, but I don't like to do it, as the dampness will make my rheumatism worse. But it can't be helped."

Well, the grasshopper didn't want to go away and leave his friend, the rabbit, all alone, but Uncle Wiggily finally persuaded him that it would be best, so the little creature hopped off and found a nice leaf. Then he curled up on the underside of it, where, in case it rained, he would not get wet, and he sang himself to sleep.

Well, now, I must tell you what happened to Uncle Wiggily.

At first he was quite lonesome, as he walked along the beach looking for a place to sleep, but then he looked up at the stars shining in the sky above him, and he saw the moon just coming up from behind the clouds, and it was shining on the ocean waves, making them look like silver, and it wasn't quite so dark then.

"I guess I will be all right," said Uncle Wiggily, bravely. "I'm not going to be afraid, for I don't believe the alligator, or fox, or bear, will come here. But I do wish I had some place where I could go in out of the dampness."

Then he suddenly thought of something.

"I know what I'll do!" he exclaimed, as he came to a pile of driftwood on the beach. "I'll make me a house of this wood, and put some seaweed on top for the roof, and in that I'll sleep as nicely as if I were at home."

Well, it didn't take Uncle Wiggily long to do this, and soon he had built as fine a little wood-and-seaweed house as heart could wish. Then he crawled inside with his crutch and his valise, and ate a small piece of cherry pie, and stretched out on some soft seaweed for his bed. In a little while he was fast, fast asleep.

Ha! But what is this funny animal crawling up along the sand with his big claws like a pair of shears which the tinsmith or the plumber uses? Eh? What's that? Why, as true as I live it's a big lobster that crawled up out of the ocean to see what he could find to eat.

Oh, Uncle Wiggily had better look out now, I tell you; hadn't he? But the poor old gentleman rabbit is still fast asleep.

The big lobster stuck out his bulgy eyes, and he moved them this way and that way, and he even looked over his shoulder with them, and then he saw the little house which the rabbit had made.

"Ha! I must see what is in that!" the lobster exclaimed and he crawled toward it. "Perhaps it is something good to eat, and I am very hungry," he said.

So the lobster looked in through the little window which Uncle Wiggily had made, and he saw the rabbit fast asleep.

"Oh, ho! Now for a good meal!" cried the lobster. Then he took one big claw and he softly pulled away some of the boards which Uncle Wiggily had used to make his house. That left a hole, and through this hole the lobster stuck his other claw, and he caught hold of the rabbit by his two ears.

"Oh! who has me? Who is it? What are you doing? Oh, my poor ears! Let go! Please let go!"

That is how Uncle Wiggily cried as he suddenly awakened.

"No, I will not!" exclaimed the lobster in a sort of a boiled-egg voice. "I'm going to crawl off with you to the bottom of the ocean!"

"Then this is the last of me and my fortune," thought the rabbit. "I might as well say good-by."

So the lobster pulled the rabbit right out of the wood-and-seaweed house, holding him by the two long ears, and he started

31

down the sandy beach with him toward the rolling, tumbling ocean. Uncle Wiggily tried to get away, but he couldn't.

Well, if you'll believe me, the big lobster nearly had the rabbit in the rolling, tumbling waves of the surf, when suddenly a flashing lantern showed glimmeringly over the sand, and a voice exclaimed:

"Shiver my timbers! If the big lobster hasn't caught a rabbit. Oh, ho! And he's trying to drown him. That will never do. I will save him. Yo ho! Heave ho!"

Uncle Wiggily looked up and he saw a big, brown, life-saving man, who was out taking a walk along the beach with a lantern to see if anybody needed to be saved. And before that lobster could drag the rabbit into the water that life guard just reached over and took the lobster up by his back, where the crawly creature couldn't pinch, and the lobster was so frightened that he let go of Uncle Wiggily's ears at once.

"Now, hop away, Mr. Rabbit," said the life guard, kindly, and you may be sure that Uncle Wiggily didn't waste any time hopping. "I'll attend to this lobster," went on the big, brown man, and then the rabbit hopped back to his wood-and-seaweed house, where he slept in peace and quietness the rest of the night. And, as for the lobster, the man put him in a pot and boiled him until he was as red as your coral necklace, or your pink necktie, and that was the end of the lobster.

So that's all to this story, if you please, but in case the clothes-wringer doesn't squeeze all the rice out of the ice-cream pudding, I'll tell you next about Uncle Wiggily and the little clam.

STORY VIII
UNCLE WIGGILY AND THE CLAM

Uncle Wiggily awakened in his wood-and-seaweed house in the morning, and he rubbed his sleepy eyes with his paws. Then he got up off his seaweed bed and as he heard a noise he exclaimed:

"Ha! That sounds like thunder. I wonder if we are going to have a storm?" And, truly, there was quite a booming and rumbling racket outside. Then the rabbit laughed at himself.

"Why, how silly of me!" he exclaimed. "That is the waves pounding on the beach. I forgot that I was at the seashore. Now I must look out and see if there are any more lobsters waiting to catch me."

Well, he was just peering out of the window, when there came a knock on the door, and Uncle Wiggily jumped back.

"My sakes alive and some baked beans!" he cried. "What's that?"

"It is only I," said a small voice. "I'm your friend, the grasshopper. How are you?"

"Oh, I'm very well, thank you," replied the rabbit. "I'm coming right out. I must tell you about the terrible time I had with the big lobster last night."

So Uncle Wiggily hopped out of the little house and told the grasshopper all about it, and the grasshopper was so frightened that he kept looking behind him all the while, for fear the lobster might be coming after him. But we all know what happened to that lobster; don't we?

"What are you going to do now?" asked the grasshopper after a while, when Uncle Wiggily was washing his face and paws, and combing out his whiskers, which had some seaweed in them.

"Oh, I am going to look for my fortune to-day," answered the rabbit. "I may find it, for I have heard that often very valuable things are cast up on the seashore by the waves. Yes, I think I

33

shall find my fortune to-day. But won't you have some breakfast, Mr. Grasshopper? I have some cherry pie left, and a few lettuce and carrot sandwiches with parsley trimmings."

"Oh, I might have a bit of parsley," spoke the jumping insect, and he ate quite a bit of it, while the rabbit ate the other things. Then they both hopped along the beach, looking for a fortune of gold or diamonds for the old gentleman rabbit.

And, just as on the other day, there were children playing in the sand, making little wells of water, and tunnels, and sandhouses, and gardens, and castles and all things like that. But there was no chest of gold, nor bag of diamonds, to be seen, though the two friends looked in every place they could think of, and in some other places, too.

"I don't believe the seashore is a very good place to find your fortune," said the rabbit, sadly, as he hopped along. And then he had to stop to take some sand out of his left ear.

"Perhaps if we ask some of the children they may be able to help us," suggested the grasshopper. Well, they did this, but, though the children were very kind, they hadn't seen any gold or diamonds, either.

"Then we'll ask some of the clams or starfish on the beach," said the grasshopper, but the clams or starfish hadn't seen anything of the rabbit's fortune, though they were very polite about it.

"Oh, I know what let's do," exclaimed the grasshopper.

"What?" asked Uncle Wiggily.

"We'll go in bathing," went on the jumping insect, "and that will cool us off, and perhaps down under the water we may find your fortune."

"The very thing," cried Uncle Wiggily; "in bathing we shall go."

Well, the old gentleman rabbit could swim a little bit, you know, and the grasshopper could float on his back as nicely as a fat man can, and together they had a very good time. It was so warm that the water didn't make Uncle Wiggily's rheumatism any worse, I'm glad to say.

Then, after a bit, the grasshopper said he thought he'd take a little hop on the sand to dry off, and that left Uncle Wiggily alone in the water. And now comes the second part of the story.

The old gentleman rabbit was swimming slowly along, looking down under the waves every once in a while to see if there was any gold on the sand beneath, when, all of a sudden, he felt something grab hold of his left hind leg.

"Oh, my! I wonder if that's the bad lobster again?" cried the rabbit, and then he saw a most curious fish, called the toggle-taggle, and this fish had hold of him.

"Oh, please let go of me!" cried the rabbit.

"No, indeed, I will not," said the toggle-taggle, speaking under water, and making a lot of bubbles come up from his breath. "I am going to drag you off to my den beneath the rocks."

"Oh, don't be so cruel!" begged the rabbit. "If you do that I can never find my fortune, and I never can go back and see Sammie and Susie Littletail again."

"That makes no difference to me at all," said the toggle-taggle, speaking in a thin, watery sort of voice, "no matter of difference at all. Here we go!" and he started to drag poor Uncle Wiggily to the bottom of the ocean, under the rocks.

"Ha! I guess I'm not going as easily as that!" cried the rabbit, and at once he began to swim as hard as he could toward land, and Uncle Wiggily could swim pretty well when he tried, let me tell you. This time he swam so hard that he pulled the toggle-taggle fish along with him, and in a second or two Uncle Wiggily was out on the sand, but the toggle-taggle still had hold of him.

"Dry land or water is all the same to me!" cried the odd fish, and then the rabbit saw that the toggle-taggle had legs, as well as fins and a tail, and so he could walk on dry land. "Now you come with me!" cried the bad fish, and he braced with his legs in the sand and was pulling the rabbit back into the water again.

"Oh, will no one help me?" cried Uncle Wiggily, for he was getting weak. And just then a little voice whispered:

35

"Turn him around, Uncle Wiggily, so I can get hold of his tail. Then I'll pinch him and make him let go of you."

"Uncle Wiggily looked, and there was a nice little clam on the sand behind the toggle-taggle, and the clam had his two shells wide open, ready to pinch the bad fish. Well, the rabbit at once began to push the toggle-taggle toward the clam, and the fish didn't know what this meant. But before he could say anything, his tail came right close to the clam's open shells, and in an instant that brave clam shut his sharp shells down very hard on the tail of the bad toggle-taggle and held on tight.

"Oh, who has me?" cried the fish, and he turned around to see what it was, and with that of course he let go of the rabbit. And then Uncle Wiggily gave a big hop and got safely away. And when the toggle-taggle saw the clam he was so frightened (for he knew that he couldn't bite through the hard shells) that the bad fish at once jumped back into the ocean, taking the brave little clam with him. But the clam didn't mind that--in fact, it was just where he wanted to go--so everything was all right.

"My! That clam saved my life, and I didn't get a chance to thank him!" said Uncle Wiggily, somewhat sadly, as he sat away up on the beach. "But I will the next time I see him." Then the grasshopper came back, and had to hear all about what had happened.

Then he and Uncle Wiggily went on looking for the fortune, and they had some more adventures before they found it.

So in the next story, if the doorknob doesn't drop off and fall into the boiled eggs, making a big white and yellow splash, I'll tell you about Uncle Wiggily and the starfish.

STORY IX
UNCLE WIGGILY AND THE STARFISH

Let me see, where did we leave off? Oh, I remember, it was where the red monkey jumped up on the elephant's back and tickled him with an ice-cream cone, wasn't it? No, I beg your pardon, I'm wrong. I promised to tell you about the old gentleman rabbit and the starfish. So if you're all ready, and are sitting comfortably, I'll begin.

It was the day after Uncle Wiggily had gotten away from the toggle-taggle fish that walked, and the little clam had pinched the bad creature on his tail. Uncle Wiggily was hopping along the sand at the seashore beach, and he was looking all around for his fortune of gold or diamonds, he didn't care much which it was, so long as he got rich and could go back home.

"I wonder what has happened to the grasshopper?" said the rabbit, for he hadn't seen the jumping insect that morning.

"Here I am," exclaimed the little chap, and with a hop he landed down beside Uncle Wiggily on the sand.

"Where have you been?" asked the rabbit. "I was beginning to think that you had left me."

"Not yet, but I am going to soon," replied the grasshopper. "You see, there is going to be a big jumping race back where I live and the hopper who jumps the farthest will get a bag of popcorn. And, as I think I will go back home to jump, I came to say good-by. Afterward, I will come here again and help you to look for your fortune."

Well, Uncle Wiggily felt a little sad to have his friend, the hoppergrass, go away, but there was no help for it. So they shook legs with each other, the grasshopper gave a big spring and a jump and away over the sea he sailed to take part in the hopping races at his home.

"Well, now, I wonder what will happen to me to-day?" thought Uncle Wiggily as he walked along the beach, looked down at the sand and listened to the waves washing up on the shore. "Perhaps I may find a bag of diamonds," he said.

And just then, if you'll believe me, he looked ahead and there, on the sand, was something that looked like a black bag, with a long, thin handle on it with which to carry it.

"Oh, ho!" exclaimed the rabbit, "I believe that is my fortune." He hopped forward, intending to pick it up, when, all of a sudden, the thing like a bag moved slowly along.

"Hum! That's queer," said the rabbit, "I never heard of a bag that could move. I must see what this is." So he went up a little closer and he saw that it wasn't a bag at all. It was a queer creature with a long sharp tail like an ice pick, or a black lead pencil, and it was crawling along, but the funny part of it was that Uncle Wiggily couldn't see any legs on which the animal walked.

"Stranger and still more strange!" exclaimed Uncle Wiggily; "what can that be?"

"If you please, I am a horseshoe crab," said a voice from under the black shell, "and if you lift me up you can see my legs."

"How shall I lift you up, Mr. Horseshoe Crab?"

"By my long tail, like an ice pick," was the answer, and when the rabbit did this, underneath a shell that was shaped somewhat like the hoof of a horse, he saw the legs of the crab. They were all covered up when the crab walked, so no one could step on his toes.

"That is very fine," said the rabbit. "Perhaps you can tell me where to find my fortune."

"I'm sorry, but I can't," said the horseshoe crab, and then he crawled on again, very slowly, and Uncle Wiggily hopped forward looking for the bag of diamonds, or gold.

Well, in a little while it got quite warm on the sandy beach, and the old gentleman rabbit felt sleepy. He yawned and he twinkled his nose like two stars on a frosty night, and then he said:

"Oh, me! Oh, my! I think I'll lie down and take a little nap on the sands." So he took some sticks and stuck them up in the beach, and over them he put some seaweed to make a shady shelter, and down under this he stretched himself out, very nice and comfortable.

Well, the first thing you know Uncle Wiggily was fast asleep. And now listen and see what happened to him. All of a sudden, up from the ocean, on her thin, kinky legs came a big sea spider, a creature something like a crab. She shot forward her big, bulgy eyes, and she saw the rabbit under the seaweed shelter.

"Ah, ha!" cried the sea spider to herself, "here is where I have a good rabbit dinner."

Slowly and softly she went on until she was quite close to the old gentleman rabbit, and Uncle Wiggily never awakened. Then the sea spider began to weave a web around the rabbit, just as a land spider weaves a web around a fly that gets into her trap. Strand after strand of the cobwebs did the sea spider throw around the sleeping rabbit, until Uncle Wiggily was as tightly fast as if he had been tied with ropes.

"Now, I'll bite him and that will be the end of him," said the sea spider, and she was just going to do this when, all of a sudden, some of the cobweb blew down and tickled Uncle Wiggily on the end of his twinkling nose, and he woke up.

"Ha! What's this?" he exclaimed, and then he found that he could not move, for he was fast in the web. "What does this mean?" he asked.

"It means that I have you!" cried the sea spider, wiggling her legs like a trolley car.

"Oh, please let me go," begged the rabbit.

"Never! Never! Never!" exclaimed the spider. Then Uncle Wiggily tried, and he tried, and he tried again, but he couldn't get loose from the web.

"Oh, will no one help me?" cried the rabbit. And just then, if you'll believe me, the waves washed something up on the sand, close to where the sea spider had Uncle Wiggily fast. And that something was a curious little fish, shaped like a star. In fact, it was a starfish with five sharp points to it. And that starfish heard Uncle Wiggily calling.

"I'll help you, Mr. Rabbit!" kindly exclaimed the fish.

"Now, you get right away from here," cried the sea spider, for well she knew that the sharp-pointed starfish could cut her cobweb in a second. "Keep away or I'll bite you!" the spider said.

"Oh, you can't scare me!" shouted the starfish. "I'm not afraid of you, and I'm going to help Uncle Wiggily." So the starfish began to roll over and over on the sand like a pinwheel, a hoop, or a wheel that has no rim, and only spokes to it. Bumpity-bump on its five points went the starfish, until it was close to Uncle Wiggily.

Then right into the sea spider's cobweb rolled the sharp-pointed starfish until, with his points, he had cut the web all to pieces and set Uncle Wiggily free, as easily as you can eat bread and jam on Saturday afternoon.

"Now you get away from here!" cried the starfish to the spider, and he threw sand at her until the crawly creature was glad enough to go back into the ocean where she belonged. And the old gentleman rabbit thanked the fish very much, and gave him a piece of lemon pie, because he was all out of the cherry kind.

"Now, I must hurry on to seek my fortune," said Uncle Wiggily, for the day was cooler now. So on he hopped, and he had another adventure.

In case the dishpan doesn't fall down off the nail, and smash the watermelon all to pieces, so there's no supper for the little mouse who lives under the ice-box, I'll tell you next about Uncle Wiggily and the slippery eel.

STORY X
UNCLE WIGGILY AND THE EEL

My, how it did rain! The water just dripped down from the clouds as if it came from a fountain turned wrong side up, and as Uncle Wiggily walked along the seashore beach, with a toadstool held over him for an umbrella he thought he had never seen such a storm.

"But, I can't stay indoors, because it rains," he said to himself as he started out that morning to look for his fortune. "That would never do. A little water can't hurt me, and besides, with this toadstool umbrella, it isn't as bad as it might be."

So he hopped along, leaning on his red-white-and-blue-striped-barber-pole crutch, and with his valise strapped to his back, and holding the toadstool umbrella over his head. And he felt so happy in spite of the rain that he sang a little song.

It went something like this, to the tune of "Hum tum-tum ti tiddle-i-um:"

"I feel so very happy,
No matter if it rains,
For I don't ride on trolley cars,
Nor yet on railroad trains.
"Whenever I feel thirsty,
I take a drink of tea,
Or, if I can't find any,
Why, milk will do for me.
"I haven't found my fortune,
Perhaps I never can,
But I can hop upon the beach,
And beat an old tin pan."

And just then the gentleman rabbit saw an old tin pan lying on the sand, and he went up to it and pounded on it with his crutch. Not hard you understand--not so hard as to hurt it, but enough to make a noise like a drum.

Uncle Wiggily and the Eel

"There, perhaps that will wake the people up," thought the rabbit for the beach was very lonesome in the rainstorm, with no children building sand houses, and no one in bathing. So Uncle Wiggily beat the tin pan again, and made a great racket, and, all of a sudden something glided out from under the pan. It was something long and thin, and it had a long, thin tail.

42

"Oh, my! It's the bad snake!" cried the rabbit, and he jumped back so quickly that he dropped his toadstool umbrella and the rain came down on the end of his twinkling nose. He was just about to hop away as fast as he could when the long, thin creature, who had been under the tin pan, exclaimed:

"I'm not a snake."

"No? Then pray tell what you are?" asked Uncle Wiggily quickly.

"I am a slippery eel," was the answer. "Just see if you can hold me, and that will show you how slippery I am."

So Uncle Wiggily very politely took hold of the eel by the tail. But, my goodness me, sakes alive and a piece of ice! In an instant that slippery eel had slipped away.

"What did I tell you?" the eel called to the rabbit, as he crawled back toward the tin.

"Well, you are certainly very slippery," said Uncle Wiggily. "I hope I didn't squeeze you too hard."

"Oh, pray do not mention it," said the eel, politely. "I am used to being squeezed, and that's why I'm so slippery; in order that I may get away easily."

"I hope I didn't wake you up from your sleep under the tin pan," went on the rabbit, who was very kind-hearted.

"Pray do not mention that, either," said the slippery eel, who was very polite. "It was time I awakened, anyhow. But, since you have been so nice about it, if ever I can do you a favor please let me know." Then he stood up on the end of his thin tail and made a low bow, and slipped into the ocean.

"Ha! That is a curious sort of chap," said Uncle Wiggily as he hopped on. "I should like to meet him again, when I have more time to talk to him. But now I must look for my fortune." So he went on looking along the beach in the rain, but never a bit of his fortune could he find.

Now, in a little while, something is going to happen. In fact it's time for it now, so I'll tell you all about it. As Uncle Wiggily was hopping along the beach, where some bushes grew close down to the water, he thought he saw something shining in the sand.

"Perhaps that may be a diamond," he said. "I'll dig it up." So he got a nice pink shell with which to dig, and he set to work, laying aside his toadstool umbrella, and not minding the rain in the least.

Then, all of a sudden, up behind the bushes came sneaking the old fuzzy fox. He had been looking all over for something to eat, but all he could find were hard shell clams, and they were too rough on his teeth, so he couldn't eat them.

"Oh, but there is a soft, delicious morsel!" exclaimed the fox, as he saw Uncle Wiggily digging in the sand, and the fox smacked his lips, and sharpened his teeth on a stone. "Now I will have a good dinner," he added.

So he crept closer and closer to Uncle Wiggily, and the old gentleman rabbit never heard him, for he was busy digging for his fortune.

"Now the thing for me to do," thought the fox, "is to spring out on him before he has a chance to move. And I think I can do it, because his back is toward me, and he can't see."

So the fox got ready to spring right on Uncle Wiggily and maybe carry him off to his den in the woods, and the old gentleman rabbit didn't know a thing about it, but kept on digging for his fortune.

"Here I go!" said the fox to himself, and he crouched down for a spring, just as your kittie does when she plays she is after a mouse. Up into the air leaped the fox, right toward the rabbit. And then, suddenly a voice cried:

"Look out, Uncle Wiggily! Look out!"

The rabbit glanced up, but he was down in the sand hole and he couldn't get out quickly on account of his rheumatism. Right toward him the fox was springing, and then, all at once, the slippery eel--for it was he who had called to the rabbit--the kind eel wiggled up out of the ocean. Up along the beach he crawled

44

quickly, until he was right in front of the rabbit in the hole. Then the eel stretched out like a piece of rope and waited.

And then the fox came down on his four feet, but, instead of landing on Uncle Wiggily he landed right on the slippery eel, and that eel was truly as slippery as a piece of ice. Right out from under him slipped the feet of the old fuzzy fox, and down he fell. Slippery, sloppery, slappery he went, sliding along on the eel until he slid all the way off and plumped into the ocean, where he was nearly drowned, for the water got in his nose and mouth and eyes.

"Now, you can get away, Uncle Wiggily," said the eel, and the rabbit kindly thanked the slippery creature, and grabbed up the shining thing he had dug out of the sand, for he thought it was a diamond. Then the fox slunk away, taking his wet and bushy tail with him, and Uncle Wiggily was safe for that time, anyhow, and the eel wiggled along after the old gentleman rabbit, who thought he had better look for a good place to sleep.

But he soon had another adventure, and I'll tell you what it was on the next page, when, in case the parlor lamp doesn't go out to a moving picture show and melt all the ice in the gas stove, the bedtime story will be about Uncle Wiggily and the horseshoe crab.

STORY XI
UNCLE WIGGILY AND THE CRAB

"My, that was a narrow escape!" said the rabbit to the slippery eel, after the fuzzy fox had gone away, as I told you in the last story. "I never can thank you enough."

"Oh, that is a mere nothing!" said the slippery eel, as he dug his tail down in the sand, modest-like. "I am always happy to do a kindness for my friends."

"You are certainly slippery," said the rabbit, "as slippery as a rubber doormat on a wet day. But look at this thing which I dug up just before the fox jumped for me. I think it is a diamond, and if it is, I will get rich, and I can go home and see my little rabbit grandchildren, Sammie and Susie Littletail." Then he held out to the slippery eel the shining object he had found in the sand.

"Alas! Alas!" sorrowfully exclaimed the eel, as he looked at the shining thing.

"What's the matter; isn't it a diamond?" asked the rabbit.

Then the slippery eel said this in a sing-song voice:

"Alas, alas,
'Tis only glass.
It is no good
To eat for food.
It will not do
For me or you.
Throw it away;
Some other day
Your fortune may
Come past your way."

"Ha, I did not know you could make up verses," said the rabbit in surprise.

"I didn't know it, either," answered the eel. "That is the first time I have ever done such a thing," and once more he dug his tail down into the sand, real modest-like and shy.

"Well, if that is only glass, instead of a diamond, I may as well throw it away," said the rabbit.

"Yes," agreed the eel, and with a flip of his tail he sent the glass spinning out into the heaving ocean.

"More bad luck for me," thought the rabbit, but he did not give up, and, bidding good-by to the slippery eel the rabbit set off down the beach to look for his fortune once more.

By this time it had stopped raining and he didn't need the toadstool umbrella, so he stuck it up in the sand in order that the next person who came along might sit under it and get out of the sun.

Well, Uncle Wiggily went on and on. He saw the children in bathing, and building sand houses, and he saw the fishermen going out to sea to catch fishes and lobsters, but still he couldn't see anything of his fortune.

Then, pretty soon, in a little while, not so very long, the old gentleman rabbit came to a place on the sand where there was a little white card. And on the card was some writing, which read:

"DIG HERE AND SEE WHAT YOU
CAN FIND."

"Ha, hum! I wonder what that means," thought Uncle Wiggily, as he sat down on the sand to rest himself. "I wonder if that can be a trick?" He had been fooled so many times that he made up his mind to be careful now. So he looked all around, but he couldn't see anything that looked like danger.

To be sure, there were some bushes up on the beach, a little way off, but there seemed to be no one in them. And there was no one on the beach near where the rabbit was.

"I guess I'll take a chance and dig," thought Uncle Wiggily. So he laid aside his valise and crutch and began to dig in the sand with a clam-shell. Deeper and deeper he went down until he began to feel something hard.

"Oh, ho!" he exclaimed. "I guess I'm getting close to it. This must be a chest of gold or diamonds that the pirates or robbers buried in the sand years ago. Now, I'll dig it up and I'll be rich. This is a lucky day for me!"

So he dug deeper and still deeper until he had partly uncovered something black and round. He thought sure it was a chest of gold, and he dug faster and faster, until all of a sudden something slipped in the sand and rolled out into the hole Uncle Wiggily had dug, and, before he knew it, he found himself slipping down and there he was, held fast by one paw, under a big black stone. It was a stone he had found under the sand and not a chest of gold at all.

At first he was too surprised to say or do anything, and then, as his foot began to pain him, he cried out:

"Oh, dear! Oh, dear! I'm caught in a trap, and I can't get out!"

"No, indeed, you can't get out!" exclaimed a voice at the edge of the hole, and, looking up, the rabbit saw a big wolf.

"Oh, did you put that card there on the sand, telling me to dig?" asked Uncle Wiggily reproachful-like.

"I did," answered the wolf, showing his teeth in a most impolite grin. "I wanted to catch you under the stone and I did. The stone rolled out of the sand when you had dug down deep enough to loosen it, and now you are fast. I'm going to jump down on you presently, and tickle you until your ribs ache."

Well, Uncle Wiggily felt pretty bad on hearing this, and he didn't know what to do. The wolf was getting ready to spring down on him, when, all at once the rabbit heard a voice whispering down to him:

"Say, Uncle Wiggily, you just ask that wolf if he is a good jumper. He'll say he is, and then you ask him if he can jump on top of the round stone he sees on the sand near the hole. He'll say he can, for he is very proud, but, instead of jumping on a stone, he'll jump on me, and then I'll stick him with my sharp tail, and he'll run away. Then I'll help you get loose."

"But who are you?" asked the rabbit, somewhat puzzled.

"I am the horseshoe crab," was the answer. "I'm up here on the sand, and I look just like a stone, and I'll pretend I really am one. The wolf can't understand my talk, so it's safe. You just ask him to jump on me."

So Uncle Wiggily looked up at the wolf, and said:

"Mr. Wolf, since you are going to tickle me anyhow, would you mind showing me what a good jumper you are before you do it?"

"Of course not!" said the wolf, who was very proud of his jumping. "I'll jump anywhere you say, and then I'll jump down and get you."

"Very well," said Uncle Wiggily, slow and sad-like, "just jump on that round stone up there on the beach, will you?"

"I will," said the wolf, and he didn't know that what he thought was a stone was only the horseshoe crab waiting to stick him with his sharp tail.

So the bad wolf gave one big jump up into the air, and down on top of the horseshoe crab he came, and the crab just stuck up his sharp pointed tail, and it tickled that wolf in the ribs so very much that the wolf had to laugh whether he wanted to or not, and he laughed so hard that he had a conniption fit, and so he couldn't get the rabbit.

Then the horseshoe crab dug away the sand around the stone, and helped Uncle Wiggily get his leg out, and the rabbit was safe, and he thanked the crab, and hopped away and the wolf didn't get him after all.

So that's all to-night, if you please, but the next Bedtime Story will be about Uncle Wiggily and the pink shell--that is if the red lobster doesn't pinch the stove's legs and make it dance a hornpipe on top of the washtubs.

STORY XII
UNCLE WIGGILY AND THE SHELL

Uncle Wiggily was lame the next day after he had been caught under the stone when the wolf nearly got him, and the horseshoe crab had dug him out. You see the stone pressed on his leg that had rheumatism in it, and it hurt the old gentleman rabbit very much.

But he was quite brave, and when he got up in the morning, even though he could hardly limp along, he decided that he would hop down the sandy beach at the seashore and see if he couldn't find his fortune there.

"It is certainly taking me quite a long time to get rich," he said to himself as he slowly moved along over the soft sand, "and perhaps I may never find any diamonds or gold. But no matter, I am enjoying myself, and that is something. Still, I would like to see Sammie and Susie Littletail again."

And when he thought of the two little rabbit children he was a bit sad. Then he decided that would never do, so he cheered himself up by singing a little song that went something like this:

"Don't be sad,
Just be glad,
For the sun is shining.
Don't be blue,
For it's true
Clouds have silver lining.
"Sing and dance,
Hop and prance,
Make some one feel jolly,
Go 'way, care,
Don't you dare
Make me melancholy."

"Ha, hum! I feel much better after that," said Uncle Wiggily, and he moved his whiskers sideways and up and down, and twinkled his nose, and then he went on looking for his fortune.

Pretty soon he came to a big snail that was crawling slowly along the beach.

"Have you seen any gold?" asked the rabbit.

"No, I am sorry to say I have not," said the snail, slowly and carefully. "But I have not gone very far this morning. I have only traveled about as far as from one orange seed to another, and that is not very far, you know. Perhaps later I may find some gold."

"Then have you seen any diamonds?" asked Uncle Wiggily.

"No, but I saw a dewdrop inside a flower sparkling in the sunshine," said the snail, "and it was brighter than a diamond."

"That is very pretty, but it is not my fortune," said the rabbit. "I must keep on." So on he went, singing his jolly song, and he kept humming it, even when the sun went behind a cloud, and it looked as if it were going to storm. The waves of the ocean grew into big billows, and they dashed up on the beach with a booming, thundering sound.

"I think we are going to have a shower," said the old gentleman rabbit. "I must look about for another toadstool umbrella." So he found one growing in the grass a little distance from the water, and he picked it. Then, strapping his valise over his shoulder, he hopped ahead, leaning on his crutch.

Pretty soon, not so very long, it began to rain. My! how the drops did come pelting down, harder and harder, but Uncle Wiggily didn't get wet because of his toadstool umbrella. And then, before you could eat a stick of peppermint candy, something hard hit the old gentleman rabbit on the nose.

"Ha! My umbrella must be leaking!" he cried. Then there came a flash of lightning, and a loud clap of thunder, and something else hit Uncle Wiggily on the end of his nose.

"Oh, I hope I'm not struck by lightning!" he cried. So he looked up, and he saw that his toadstool umbrella was full of holes, and the reason of this was that it was hailing instead of raining. The rain drops had turned into little round chunks of ice, just like white pebbles, and they were pelting down, and had torn the rabbit's umbrella all to pieces.

"Whatever shall I do?" cried Uncle Wiggily, as he tossed aside the toadstool. "That is of no use to me now, and there is no place where I can go to get in out of the rain. Oh, my! How those hailstones hurt!" And indeed they did, for they were as large as bird's eggs now, and they were bouncing down all over, and hitting Uncle Wiggily on his ears and nose and all over.

He tried to hold his crutch over his head, but that did no good, and then he tried to hold up his valise with the cherry pie in it to shelter himself, but that did no good, either.

"Oh, I'll be knocked to pieces by the hailstones!" the rabbit cried. "Where can I go? Oh, if I only had a shell house such as the snail carries on her back, I would be all right."

"Here is a house for you!" cried a little voice, and looking to one side Uncle Wiggily saw his old friend the grasshopper, and that grasshopper was beneath a big pink shell that was on the beach, with one edge raised up like a shed. "Crawl under the shell, and the hailstone can't hurt you!" went on the hoppergrass. "This pink shell is the best kind of a house."

"Well, I do declare--so it is!" agreed Uncle Wiggily, and he lost no time in crawling under the pink shell which was just the color of baby's cheeks. Then how the hailstones did rattle down on that shell! It was just like peas or dried corn falling into a tin pan. Rattle-te-bang! Rattle-te-bang! went the hailstones, but they couldn't hurt the grasshopper or Uncle Wiggily now, for the chunks of ice hit on the hard shell and burst to pieces.

Then, all of a sudden Uncle Wiggily heard some one crying. Oh, it was such a sad, pitiful voice.

"Oh, what shall I do? Where can I go?" wailed the voice.

"Some one needs help," said the rabbit quickly.

"Maybe it's a bear," suggested the hoppergrass.

"Nonsensicalness!" exclaimed the rabbit. "I'm going to look out." So he peered out from under the edge of the big pink shell, and he saw a little baby crab crawling along with a basket of seapeanuts in little bags on one claw.

"Oh, I'm so miserable!" cried the little crab. "I started out to sell peanuts, but the hailstones burst the bags open, and the peanuts came out and they're all wet, and no one will buy wet peanuts. What shall I do?"

"Come right in here," said Uncle Wiggily kindly. "We'll help you." So the little crab crawled beneath the pink shell, where the hailstones couldn't hit him, and when the storm was over the old gentleman rabbit and the grasshopper built a fire, and they dried out the peanuts. Then the grasshopper took some of his molasses and he glued the torn bags together, and Uncle Wiggily put back the dry peanuts in them, and then the little crab went off very happy, indeed, and sold them for a penny a bag.

"Ha! The pink shell did us a great kindness," said the old gentleman rabbit, as he hopped out. "Now I will look once more for my fortune." Then the grasshopper flew away over the sea again and the rabbit went on alone, eating a few peanuts the baby crab had given him.

And he soon had another adventure. What it was I'll tell you soon, for the story will be about Uncle Wiggily and the fiddler--that is, if the piano stool doesn't turn into a merry-go-'round and whirl about so fast that it makes the milk bottle dizzy.

STORY XIII
UNCLE WIGGILY AND THE FIDDLER

It was the day after Uncle Wiggily had taken shelter under the pink shell when the hailstones came down, and the old gentleman rabbit was walking along the sandy beach, looking to see what he could see.

"You never can tell when you are going to find your fortune in this world," he said, "and I may come upon mine any moment. So I must be ready for it." Then he went on a little farther, and he felt hungry. "Perhaps there is a bit of cherry pie still in my valise," he said. So he looked, and, sure enough, there was some pie, and he ate it.

It was nearly all gone, and there were only a few crumbs of the pie left, when the old gentleman rabbit heard some one say:

"Oh, how hungry I am! Oh, if I only had something to eat. I wonder where I can find anything?"

Then the rabbit looked down, and there was the slow-crawling snail, looking very hungry indeed.

"Oh, ho! So it's you, is it?" asked the rabbit. "Why, it seems to me you are not very far from the place where I last saw you."

"That is so, I am not," answered the snail. "You see I go very slowly and in a whole day I only moved about as far as an ice-cream cone. I have been looking for something to eat, but I can't find it."

"Oh, I'll gladly give you what I have left," spoke Uncle Wiggily, as he scattered the crumbs of the cherry pie about, and the snail ate them all up.

"I don't s'pose you have seen anything of my fortune, have you?" asked the rabbit, as he wiped his whiskers on a red napkin, and closed up his valise.

"No, I haven't," said the snail. "But I will tell you something I overheard to-day and perhaps that will help you. As I was crawling slowly along I heard two sand fleas talking together. One said to the other that there was going to be a grand dance of all the sand fleas on the beach to-night and that there would be plenty of gold and diamonds at the party. Perhaps if you went to it you might find your fortune--that is, if some one had any gold or diamonds they didn't want."

"That's a good idea," said the rabbit. "I'll be there, and I'm much obliged to you for telling me. Where do the sand fleas hold their dance?"

"Down on the beach by the wreck of the old sailing ship," answered the snail. "Be there at the hour of midnight, and I hope you will find your fortune."

"I'll be there," said the rabbit. "Oh, I'll be there."

Then the snail crawled away, and Uncle Wiggily hopped along on the sand, but he didn't look for his fortune as he thought he would find it at the fleas' party.

"Since I am going to be up quite late to-night," he said, "I had better take a little sleep now." So he stretched out under some seaweed that he laid over some driftwood for a shady shelter and soon he was fast asleep. Then, after a while, he awakened and ate his supper and soon it was midnight, and he set off toward the place where the wreck of the old ship was on the beach, for there the sand fleas were to have their hop and dance.

As he came near the place, the old gentleman rabbit heard laughter and talking, and he saw tiny lights flitting about. Then he came still nearer, and he saw a most curious sight. All around in the sand were little pieces of wood, set in a circle, and on each piece of wood was a lightning bug. They lighted up the place like small electric lanterns.

There was a large circle of sand, and inside of that was the ballroom where the dance was to take place. It was all decorated with seaweed and moss, and it looked very pretty with lightning bugs scattered here and there in the green drapery like fairy lights.

And then the sand fleas! Oh, there were hundreds of them, and they were hopping all about, sometimes over each other's backs and around corners and through the middle, while some even turned somersaults, and they were having a glorious time.

"I wonder when the dance is going to begin?" thought Uncle Wiggily. "I wish it would soon start, for I see that these fleas have on many diamonds, and they also have lots of gold in their pockets. Perhaps, when they dance they will drop some of the gold and diamonds, and, in case they don't want them, I can pick them up and have them for my fortune."

Then, all of a sudden, some of the fleas began to cry out:

"Where is the music? Why doesn't the music start, so that we can dance?"

And surely enough, there was no music for the party. Then a big gray flea called out:

"Alas, and lack-a-day! We will have no music! I had hired a dozen Katy-Dids and a dozen Katy-Didn'ts to come and play for us, but they have just telephoned that they can't come, as their legs are stiff. So we can have no dance, as we have no music."

"Oh, how perfectly dreadful!" cried a blue lady flea.

And just then some of the other fleas saw Uncle Wiggily looking in at them from behind the old wrecked ship.

"Perhaps the rabbit can play for us," said some of the fleas. "Can you, Mr. Rabbit?"

"No, I can't," he said, and he felt very sorry for them. "But I will see if I can find some one who can," for Uncle Wiggily was very kind-hearted, and always did what he could to help.

So he strolled down the beach looking for some one to play for the sand fleas. And as he walked along he met a fiddler crab, which is a crab with very long legs. And as soon as he saw that fiddler crab Uncle Wiggily knew that the long-legged creature could make music.

"Will you come and play for the fleas' party?" asked the rabbit. "I will make a fiddle out of my crutch and some seaweed for strings, and you can play it."

"I will," said the fiddler crab, kindly, "but who will play the drum? We need a drum. Who will play it?"

"I would if I had a drum," said the rabbit, bravely.

"I'll be the drum," suddenly cried a voice, and up from the ocean popped a fish called the puff fish or sea robin, and he can make himself look like a blown-up paper bag full of wind. "I'll be the drum and you can make me go 'Boom! Boom!'" said the blow-fish.

"Fine!" cried Uncle Wiggily. "Come on back to the sand fleas' party with me." So the fiddler crab and the drum fish went along. Then the rabbit soon made a fiddle, with seaweed for strings, and the fiddler crab played it with his long legs, making tunes like "Please Buy Me an Ice-Cream Cone and Take Me on the Merry-go-'Round."

And the drum fish puffed himself up like a balloon, and Uncle Wiggily beat him with a soft stick, and there was fine music. Then the sand fleas hopped and danced about until they could hop and dance no more.

But they didn't drop any gold or diamonds, and, when the party was over, the rabbit was as poor as when it started. But still he didn't mind. Then he went to sleep under a pile of seaweed, while the sea robin and the fiddler crab went home in the ocean.

And on the next page, in case the egg beater doesn't get stuck on the rolling-pin and make the pie crust fall through the nutmeg grater, I'll tell you about Uncle Wiggily and the watermelon.

STORY XIV
UNCLE WIGGILY AND THE WATERMELON

"Well," asked the slow snail of Uncle Wiggily, as he met the old gentleman rabbit on the beach next day, "did you get any of your fortune at the fleas' party?"

"None at all," answered the old gentleman rabbit. "There was plenty of gold and diamonds to be seen, but the fleas didn't give me any."

"Perhaps they forgot it?" suggested the snail. "Some of the fleas are very forgetful. I once knew one whose mother sent him to the store for a pound of sugar and a quart of milk, and what do you s'pose he bought?"

"I don't know," answered the rabbit, curious-like.

"He got a pound of milk and a quart of sugar, and the milk all ran out of the paper bag in which the groceryman put it, and the sugar stuck fast to the milk pail, and they had a dreadful time getting it out. That shows you what a flea will do sometimes. Perhaps if you ask them for your fortune they will give it to you."

"I'll do it the next time I meet one," decided Uncle Wiggily. "But now I must go on and look for myself."

"Wait until I sing a little song for you," said the slow snail, and he hummed this song very, very slowly:

"When I am in a hurry
I slowly crawl along,
And when I finish crawling
I sing a little song.
"For if I hurried too much
I'd get there all too soon,
Though some day I am going
To climb up to the moon.
"And then when I get up there
I'll sleep the whole long day,

58

Or crawl upon the moonbeams,
Or jump into the hay."

"Ha! hum!" exclaimed Uncle Wiggily. "That's a very good song, and I'm sure it will help me find my fortune. Now I must say good-by and travel along."

Uncle Wiggily and the Watermelon

"If you will wait I'll come with you," spoke the snail. "But then I s'pose you are in a hurry, Uncle Wiggily, and I go too slow for you."

"That's it," said the rabbit kindly, and he gave one big hop that carried him twice as far as the snail could travel in a week of Sundays without counting Christmas.

Well, it wasn't very long after this before Uncle Wiggily got to the top of a hill. When he started to climb up from the bottom he thought perhaps there might be gold at the top, but when he did get to the summit all he found there was a big green thing, with stripes on.

"I wonder what this can be?" thought the rabbit. "It looks like a baseball, and yet it's too large for that, and besides it isn't quite round. And, once more, it's green instead of white, for all baseballs are white. Ha! I know what it is. That must be a football which the boys kick about. I guess I'll kick it. Perhaps there may be gold inside."

So he got ready to kick it, but you know how it is with old gentlemen rabbits who have the rheumatism and have to go about on a crutch. As soon as Uncle Wiggily lifted up one foot-- the one that had no rheumatism in it--and when he leaned on his crutch, the crutch suddenly slipped, and down he went ker-flumux ker-flimix all in a heap.

"Well, here's a pretty kettle of fish!" he cried. "I ought never to have tried to kick that green football. I should have waited until it was ripe."

So he sat down on top of the hill, and looked at the ocean tumbling and foaming on the beach below him, and he waited for the green football to get ripe. And, every once in a while he would poke it with his crutch to see if it was getting soft, but it wasn't.

And once, right after he did this, the old gentleman rabbit heard some one cry out:

"My goodness, Uncle Wiggily! What are you doing?"

"Waiting for this green football to get ripe so that I can kick it," was the rabbit's reply.

"Oh, ho! Oh, ha!" laughed the grasshopper for it was that leaping insect who had spoken, "that is not a football, it is a watermelon, and inside it is all red and sweet and juicy. Come, if you can, cut it open, we will have a fine feast. I haven't had any watermelon in some time. Can you cut it?"

"Oh, I can cut it fast enough," declared the rabbit. "Here goes, and I hope it is better looking on the inside than it is on the outside."

So the rabbit took out his knife, with which he usually spread his bread and butter, and he cut a hole in the watermelon. Then Uncle Wiggily and the grasshopper scooped out all the nice, red, juicy part and ate it.

And, would you ever believe it? Something happened right after that. They had no sooner wiped the red watermelon juice off their faces than there was a terrible roaring sound in the bushes, and out jumped a big black bear. Oh, he was going on something frightful, yes, really he was, but don't be frightened, for I won't let him hurt anybody. I'll let him chew on my typewriter first and that will dull his teeth. On the bear came, straight for the watermelon.

"Oh, what can I do?" cried Uncle Wiggily. "That bear will get me, but he won't hurt you, Mr. Grasshopper, as you are so small."

"Don't worry," said the hoppergrass, kindly. "I'll find a way to save you. Quick! Before the bear sees you, hop inside the watermelon," for you see they had eaten up all the inside, and left the melon rind hollow, just like a yellow pumpkin Jack-o'-lantern, at Hallowe'en.

Uncle Wiggily saw that this was the best thing to do, so inside the melon he hopped, and then the grasshopper put back in place the piece they had cut out, and you never would have known but that the melon was a whole, new one, never having been cut and the inside eaten out.

On came the bear, sniffing with his black nose. Then he saw the grasshopper and asked, suspicious-like:

"Is there a rabbit around here?"

"I don't see any," spoke the grasshopper, and he really couldn't see any one but the bear because Uncle Wiggily was inside the melon, you know.

"Well, if there is no rabbit I'll have to eat this watermelon, then," said the bear, "for I am very hungry."

Now the grasshopper knew that if the bear once bit into the melon and opened it, he'd see the rabbit hiding inside. So what did the hoppergrass do but give the melon a shove with his strong hind legs, and down the hill the melon rolled, with the rabbit in it, just as Buddy Pigg, the guinea pig boy, once rolled down hill inside a cabbage.

Faster and faster down the hill rolled the melon, with Uncle Wiggily in it, and then the bear saw one of the rabbit's paws sticking out of a crack.

"Oh, ho! You have fooled me!" cried the bear to the grasshopper. "Now, I'll chase after that melon and get the rabbit, too!"

So the bear started down the hill after the melon, but his foot slipped and he slid down, oh, so fast, that he got to the bottom of the hill first. There he stood waiting for Uncle Wiggily. But a queer thing happened. The melon hit a stone, burst open and out flew the rabbit on a pile of soft sand. But the pieces of the melon hit the bear on his soft and tender nose, and he thought he was surely killed, and off he ran to the woods howling and growling. So that's how Uncle Wiggily escaped from the bear, for the old gentleman rabbit wasn't hurt a bit for all his tumble.

Then he washed the pieces of melon off his clothes, and traveled on again, with the grasshopper, to seek his fortune. And he had another advantage soon. I'll tell you about it very shortly, when, in case the ice man doesn't go skating and forget to leave us a loaf of bread, the next Bedtime story will be about Uncle Wiggily and the Katy-Did.

STORY XV
UNCLE WIGGILY AND KATE-DID

"Well, what are we going to do to-day?" asked the grasshopper of Uncle Wiggily, as they sat down to breakfast one sunny morning, after a rain the night before.

"Oh, I suppose I must keep on searching for some gold or diamonds for my fortune," answered the old gentleman rabbit. "But I am getting quite tired of going around so much and finding nothing. I'll keep it up a week or so longer, and then, if I don't find any money, I'm going back home, anyhow. I'm quite lonesome for Sammie and Susie Littletail and all of my friends."

"When you go home I hope that I can go with you," said the grasshopper sort of sad-like. "I'll be sorry when you leave me."

"Of course you can come along," answered Uncle Wiggily, kindly, as he flopped his long ears back and forth.

Then he and the grasshopper finished their breakfast, washed the acorn cups and saucers, and shook the crumbs off the green leaf which they had used for a table cloth. And pretty soon a whole lot of little black ants crawled along and ate up all the crumbs, so that nothing was wasted.

"Well, here we go!" cried the old gentleman rabbit cheerfully as he picked up his barber-pole crutch and slung his valise over his shoulder. Then he hopped off and so did the grasshopper, singing a funny little song on the way, and also playing the fiddle with his left hind leg. The song went something like this:

"Here we go,
Fast and slow,
Hopping on our way.
In heat and cold
We look for gold,
Which we may find some day.
"Sing a song

Not too long,
Cheerful, gay and bright.
When wide awake
We eat sweet cake,
And then we sleep all night.
"Hipping, hopping,
Without stopping
We sing and do not cry.
Skip and jump
Around the pump;
Now we'll say good-by."

"Why, what in the world did you say that for?" asked Uncle Wiggily of the grasshopper as the insect finished his song. "There is no one here to whom we can say good-by, and not a sign of a pump."

"I know it, but you see I'm just making believe," replied the cheerful little fellow, turning one somersault and part of another one.

"Oh, then that's different," agreed the old gentleman rabbit, as he stooped over to take a stone out of his shoe. And, just as he did so there came bouncing down out of a tall tree a big green hickory nut, and it almost hit Uncle Wiggily on the end of his twinkling nose.

"Hum!" exclaimed the grasshopper, as he crawled under a big leaf in order to be out of danger, "some one is throwing things at us. I wonder who it can be?"

"I don't know," answered the rabbit, and then he and the grasshopper looked up in a tree, but they could see no one. So they went on a little farther, and pretty soon Uncle Wiggily got another stone in his shoe. He stooped over to take it out when slam-bang! down came a green butternut this time, and it struck him on the end of his left ear.

"This must stop!" cried the old gentleman rabbit. "If it doesn't, the first thing we know there will be cocoanuts falling down on us and then we will be hurt."

"Oh, I think there are no monkeys around here to throw cocoanuts at us," said the grasshopper, "but this is certainly very strange. Perhaps it is the alligator or the fuzzy fox up in a tree trying to hurt us by throwing the little nuts."

"Perhaps," agreed Uncle Wiggily. "Well, we will hurry on, and get out of these woods." So they hurried all they could, but as it happened the grasshopper got a big wooden splinter in his left front leg and it took him and Uncle Wiggily quite a while to get it out, and when at last they did so, it was almost night.

They were hopping along, looking for a place to sleep in the woods, when all of a sudden down came a big black walnut, and it hit Uncle Wiggily's crutch, bouncing off with a bang.

"Who did that?" cried the rabbit looking up as well as he could in the darkness. "Who threw that nut?"

"Katy did!" cried a shrill voice up in a tree. "Katy did!"

"Oh, she did; eh?" exclaimed the old gentleman rabbit. "Well I always thought Katy was a nice little girl. I can't believe she'd throw anything at me. It's not possible!"

"Katy did--she did!" cried the voice in the tree again.

"Oh, would you ever think such a thing of her?" asked the grasshopper, who was quite excited.

"No, I wouldn't," declared Uncle Wiggily sad-like. "Where does Katy live?" he went on. "Perhaps if I speak to her, and tell her how unpleasant it is to have nuts thrown at one she won't do it again. Where does she live?"

"Katy did! Katy did! Katy did!" was all the voice said.

"Of course! I know that by this time," said Uncle Wiggily. "But where does she live? Whereabouts in these woods?"

"Katy did! Katy did!" cried the voice again.

"Ah, I see!" exclaimed the grasshopper, "That means she once did live here, but that she has moved away. That must be it."

"Then I'm glad of it," spoke the rabbit. "I hope she doesn't come back to throw any more things at us. Do you think she will?" and he looked up in the tree to see who had been talking so about Katy.

"Katy did! Katy did!" was all the answer there was.

But all of a sudden there was a rustling in the bushes, and out into the moonlight, which was then shining in the forest, there came a little white pussy cat, with four legs and a long tail.

"Oh, dear!" she cried. "I'm Katy, and I heard what you all said about me. But I didn't do it at all. I didn't throw a thing at you, Uncle Wiggily, or at the grasshopper either. I wouldn't do such a thing. Oh, how can you believe it? I didn't do it at all."

"Katy did! Katy did!" cried the shrill voice up in the tree-top. "Katy did--she did!"

"Ha, hum!" cried the old gentleman rabbit. "This must be looked into. If Katy didn't do it, we mustn't have her talked about that way. Come, Mr. Grasshopper, we'll see who's calling out about Katy so much."

But just as the rabbit was helping the grasshopper to climb up the tree, to see who it was that had been calling, all of a sudden out from behind a stump there sprang a savage fox, who wanted to eat up Uncle Wiggily and the pussy and the grasshopper also. But the rabbit happened to see a hole in the ground.

"Quick! Jump down here all of you!" he cried and he helped the pussy and the grasshopper to get into the hole where they would be safe from the fox. And, as they disappeared under ground the voice up in the tree-top cried once more:

"Katy did! Katy did!"

"Oh, ho! I'll put a stop to that to-morrow!" declared Uncle Wiggily. "Don't cry, Katy, dear. I'll see that whoever is bothering you will stop." Then the little white pussy dried her tears, and the three friends slept safely in the hole all night, and the fox did not bother them a bit.

And the next day Uncle Wiggily found out who was calling to Katy, and who threw the nuts at him, and I'll tell you about it on the next page, when the story will be about Uncle Wiggily and

Katy-Didn't--that is, if the trolley car doesn't run up on the front stoop and break the rocking chair's arms so I can't sing the rag doll to sleep.

STORY XVI
UNCLE WIGGILY AND KATY-DIDN'T

Katy, the nice little white pussy, was the first one to awaken the next morning in the hole where she and Uncle Wiggily and the grasshopper had crawled to get away from the bad fox. Katy arose, washed her face and her paws with her red tongue, and then she softly tickled the grasshopper on his nose with the end of her fuzzy-wuzzy tail.

"Ha, ho! What's the matter?" cried the grasshopper, as he hopped out of the bed made of dried leaves. "Is the house on fire?"

"No, we're not in a house, but in a hole under ground so I don't very well see how it could catch on fire," spoke Katy. "I wanted you to get up and help me with the breakfast. I thought we would let Uncle Wiggily sleep late this morning, as he is tired."

"That's a good idea," declared the little jumping chap. "I'll just take a hop outside and see what I can find to eat."

Well, the grasshopper started to go out of the hole, leaving Uncle Wiggily fast asleep, but, all of a sudden the tiny jumping fellow came back, and, instead of being green, as he usually was, he had turned quite pale.

"What's the matter?" asked Katy.

"The hole is stopped up!" cried the grasshopper. "Some one has filled up the front door with dirt and we can't get out."

"Oh, that's too bad!" said the pussy, and she and the grasshopper looked at the lightning bug, who was shining brightly like a Christmas tree-candle down in the dark hole so they could see. He had shone all night for them. "How will we ever get out?" went on the pussy. "It is terrible to be shut up here."

"What's that? Is there more trouble?" suddenly asked Uncle Wiggily, as he got out of bed feet first.

"Yes," said the grasshopper, "the front door of the hole is stopped up, and we can't get out. I think the bad fox did it."

"Very likely," agreed Uncle Wiggily. "But don't worry, for I can easily dig out the dirt, and then we can go up and find out who it was that said Katy threw nuts at us when she didn't."

So Uncle Wiggily went to the front door of the hole-house and began to dig with his strong feet. And then he happened to think of something.

"If I dig a new front door near the place where the fox stopped up the old one," said the old gentleman rabbit thoughtful-like, "that bad creature may be there waiting to grab us when we go out. So I'll play a trick on him. I'll dig a new door for this hole-house and we'll go out that way. I'll dig it at the back."

So Uncle Wiggily did this and soon there was a nice opening from the hole underground, and it was some distance away from the one by which the three friends had gone in. And, surely enough, they looked through the trees when they went out, and there was that bad fox near the stopped-up hole, waiting for them to come out so that he might grab them.

"I guess he'll wait there a long while for us," said Uncle Wiggily, blinking his nose, and laughing. "Come on now, very quietly and we'll go off in the woods where he can't find us." So away through the forest they went, and the fox never saw them. He stayed by the hole, which he had stopped up with dirt and stones, and he was there a week, waiting for the rabbit and his friends to come up. And the fox got so thin from having nothing to eat in all that time that when he finally did go away his tail nearly dropped off and blew away.

But Uncle Wiggily, and the grasshopper, and the pussy whose name was Katy traveled on and on. Over the hills they went, and through the fields, but they couldn't find out who it was that had said Katy had thrown the nuts when she didn't do it at all.

At last they came to another forest, and just as night was coming on, and Uncle Wiggily was passing under a tree, slam-bang! down came another butternut, and nearly hit him on the eye.

"There! You see, I didn't throw that," cried Katy, who was walking beside Uncle Wiggily.

"Yes, it couldn't have been you," agreed the old gentleman rabbit. "I wonder who did it?"

"Katy did! Katy did!" suddenly cried a voice.

"No, she didn't," said Uncle Wiggily, firmly. "Who are you to say such things?"

"Here he is--I see him!" exclaimed the grasshopper. "It isn't any one at all--it's a little green bug with wings, and he is something like me. He's been saying that 'Katy did' when she didn't do it at all."

And, sure enough, there on a tree was a little light-green bug, and, as Uncle Wiggily watched, he heard this insect call out as bold as bold could be:

"Katy did! Katy did!"

"Now look here!" said the old gentleman rabbit, and he pointed his long ears and his crutch at the green bug, "why do you say such things when you know they aren't so? Katy never threw any nuts at me--they just dropped down off the tree themselves. I'm sure of it. Katy never did it, and she feels badly to have you say so."

"Katy did! Katy did!" cried the insect again, as if he hadn't heard the rabbit speak. "I have to say it, you know," he went on, as he scraped his two long hind legs together. "I have to call out that Katy did, Uncle Wiggily."

"You do? Even when she didn't do it?" asked the rabbit, surprised-like.

"Yes," said the insect. "Katy did! Katy did! I have to call--Katy did."

"Oh, I think it's just too horrid for anything!" said poor Katy, almost ready to cry.

"I wish you wouldn't say such things about a nice pussy," spoke the grasshopper. "For Katy didn't do it. I know she didn't."

And just then, off in another tree, there came a second voice calling:

"Katy didn't! Katy didn't!"

"There, I knew some one would be kind to me!" exclaimed the pussy. "Some one knows I didn't do it. I didn't throw the nuts."

"Katy did! Katy did!" cried the first green insect.

"Katy didn't! Katy didn't!" answered the second little green chap.

"She did!" went on the first one.

"She didn't! Katy didn't!" answered his brother, positive-like.

"Katy did!" "Katy didn't!"

"Oh, my, this dispute is very unpleasant!" said Uncle Wiggily. "Please stop it." But the green insects wouldn't stop, and they kept on calling. First one would say that Katy did do it and then the other would say she didn't, and so they went on:

"Katy did!" "Katy didn't!"

"Well," said Uncle Wiggily at last, when he had tried to make them stop disputing, but couldn't do it, "at any rate, Katy, you have some friends who will stand up for you, and who will always say you didn't do it, and I know you didn't, no matter if the others say you did. Now let's find a place to sleep, and to-morrow I will once more look for my fortune."

So they found a nice hollow stump in which to sleep, and nothing happened to them all night, except that a big-eyed, feathery owl tried to bite the grasshopper. But Uncle Wiggily tickled the bad bird with his crutch and made him fly away, and then they all slept in peace and quietness until morning.

The next day the old gentleman rabbit had quite an adventure. I'll tell you what it was in the following Bedtime Story which will be about Uncle Wiggily and Peetie Bow Wow--that is, if my piece of huckleberry pie doesn't fall into the milk pitcher and turn it sky-blue-pink like the elephant's lemonade at the circus.

STORY XVII
UNCLE WIGGILY AND PEETIE

Katy, the little white pussy, felt quite happy the next day, after she and Uncle Wiggily and the grasshopper had slept in the hollow stump, as I told you last.

"No matter if some of the green insects do say I did throw those nuts," she said, "others of them will say I didn't do it, so it will be all right." And from then on, even up to the present time, you can hear the did and the didn't insects calling to each other in the cool night:

"Katy did!" "Katy didn't!" That's how they dispute, and they never seem to settle it.

"Where are you going?" asked the old gentleman rabbit as he saw the pussy starting off by herself in the woods, when breakfast was over.

"Oh, I am going back home," she said. "I have been away too long already, and my mamma will be worried about me. But I am very glad to have met you and the grasshopper, and I hope you will soon find your fortune, Uncle Wiggily."

"I hope so too," spoke the rabbit, and then he and the grasshopper started off together through the woods, looking on all sides for any signs of gold or diamonds.

They traveled on for many miles, but I'm sorry to say they didn't find any fortune at all--not even so much as a five-cent piece with a hole in it. When noon came they sat down by a little spring of water and built a fire. Then the rabbit roasted some carrots and the grasshopper ate a small piece of cherry pie, and some bread and jam, for he was very fond of sweet things.

"Well, we'll travel on again," said the rabbit, as he scattered the crumbs for the ants to eat.

"Why don't you stay here and look for your fortune?" asked the grasshopper, wiggling his ears.

"Oh, it would be of no use," said Uncle Wiggily. "Haven't we looked all over in these woods? And we didn't even find a diamond ring. No, we must travel on."

"Why don't you dig a hole here by this old stump?" asked the grasshopper. "Perhaps there is a gold mine here. It is nice and shady, and you can dig deep and keep cool. I will sit on the stump and watch you, and also sing a song now and then."

"Perhaps that will be a good plan," agreed Uncle Wiggily, after thinking it over. "I believe I will dig here. It can do no harm and it may be of some use." So, laying aside his crutch and his valise, he began to dig in the earth with his sharp feet.

"My! I'm making a regular mine!" thought Uncle Wiggily, after a while. "But there doesn't seem to be any gold here. However, I'll go down a little deeper."

And then, all of a sudden he heard the grasshopper cry:

"Look out, Uncle Wiggily! Look out! The alligator is coming!"

"Oh, me! Oh, my!" shouted the rabbit, as he tried to jump up out of the hole he had dug. But it was too deep and he only fell back to the bottom. He heard the whirr of the grasshopper's wings as that hopping chap flew away, and as the grasshopper skipped over the daisies he cried out:

"I'll go get help, Uncle Wiggily!" for he knew he couldn't fight the alligator all alone.

"Oh, whatever shall I do?" thought the rabbit. "I must get out." So he gave another jump, but it was of no use, and then before Uncle Wiggily could twinkle his nose twice, over the edge of the hole leaned the skillery-scalery alligator.

"Ah, ho! So there you are!" cried the scaly creature, smiling such a big smile that it is a wonder the top of his head didn't fly off. "So you are in a hole? Well, that suits me, for you can't get away, and I can take you whenever I please. I guess I'll wait until I am a little more hungry. Meanwhile I'll sit here and look at you."

And the alligator did this, perched on the edge of the hole, with his mouth grinning from ear to ear and his tail slowly switching to and fro, to keep off the flies from his scaly hide.

"Are you really going to bite me?" asked the rabbit, sad-like.

"I am," replied the alligator, in a nutmeg-grater voice.

"Would you let me go if I gave you my barber-pole crutch and my valise filled with cherry pie?" asked Uncle Wiggily, sorrowful-like.

"Not for worlds!" cried the alligator, smacking his jaws. "I'm going to bite you now." And with that he started to crawl down into the hole to get the rabbit.

But don't worry. Some one is on the way to save Uncle Wiggily. All of a sudden, just as the alligator was almost down to Uncle Wiggily, and only the tip of his tail was sticking out over the edge, there was a movement on the other side of the hole, and, looking up, the rabbit saw a curious sight.

There was some sort of an animal peering down at him. But such an animal! His tail was all stuck up with stickery burrs, and it had a lump of mud on the end. On one ear was stuck a big green leaf, and on the other ear was a piece of red paper from a Chinese lantern. And on his back were chestnut burrs and bits of briar bushes; and this animal grinned and showed his teeth and shook himself so that mud was scattered all over. Then this animal cried:

"Here, you bad alligator! Get away and let that rabbit alone!"

"What for; do you want to bite him yourself?" asked the skillery-scalery alligator creature, grinning from ear to ear.

"No, I don't," answered the dreadful looking animal. "But you get away from here or I'll eat you!" And, my! you should have heard that muddy creature growl. No, perhaps it's just as well you didn't hear him, or you might have bad dreams. Anyhow, that new, queer animal growled so that even the alligator was frightened, and Uncle Wiggily said to himself:

"Oh, worse and worse! If the alligator doesn't get me this terrible creature will!"

Then the terrible creature growled some more and showed his teeth and the alligator crawled out of the hole and scurried away, taking his scaly tail with him.

"Ha! Ha! That's the time I fooled you!" cried the terrible looking animal, and then he burst out laughing and took the paper and leaf from his ears, shook out the burrs from his tail, and whom do you s'pose it was? Why none other than Peetie Bow Wow, the nice puppy dog.

"Oh, you saved my life!" cried Uncle Wiggily, thankfully.

"Yes, he certainly did," said the grasshopper, perching himself on the edge of the hole. "I met Peetie in the woods and told him about you, and he rolled in the mud and water and stuck himself all up with burrs, so as to make himself look as terrible as possible and scare the alligator. It was a good trick; wasn't it?"

"It was, indeed!" cried the rabbit, as the grasshopper and the puppy dog helped him out of the hole; "even if I didn't find my fortune."

So the alligator didn't get the rabbit, and Uncle Wiggily had another adventure next day. I'll tell you what it was very soon for the following story will be about Uncle Wiggily and Jackie Bow-Wow--that is, if the picture on the wall doesn't turn upside down and scare the parlor lamp so that it goes out on the porch to sit on the door mat.

STORY XVIII
UNCLE WIGGILY AND JACKIE

Uncle Wiggily, with the grasshopper, and Peetie Bow-Wow, the little puppy dog, were traveling along the road together, and the old gentleman rabbit was looking on both sides for his fortune. It was the day after Peetie had saved Uncle Wiggily from the bad alligator, and the three friends had spent the night in a hollow stump in the woods. Then they had breakfast, eating some cherry pie that the rabbit had left in his valise.

"Tell me, Peetie," said Uncle Wiggily, as they tramped along, "how does it happen that you are so far from home; and what were you doing in the woods just before you scared the alligator away?"

"Oh, my brother Jackie and I came to visit our grandpa, who lives somewhere around here," said the puppy dog. "Yesterday Jackie and I went for a walk in the woods, and I got lost. It was then that the grasshopper found me and asked me to come and help you."

"Which you kindly did," said the old gentleman rabbit, as he brushed a mosquito off his twinkling nose. "But I didn't know you were lost, Peetie. Why didn't you say something about it? And here you've been away from your grandpa's house all night and he and your brother Jackie may be very much worried. Why didn't you tell me about this yesterday?"

"Well, I thought you had troubles enough of your own," said Peetie politely, as he looked down in a puddle of water to see if his tail was fastened on straight. "But I would like very much, Uncle Wiggily, to find my way back to grandpa's house, and see Jackie," he went on. "And I know he'll be glad to see you."

"Then we must start off at once and look for your grandpa's house," decided the old gentleman rabbit. "I will let my fortune go for to-day, and we will take care of you."

So off they started, looking for the house of Peetie's grandpa. The puppy dog helped them look, of course, but he was too small to be of much use. Every once in a while he would find a nice juicy bone, and he would stop to gnaw that instead of looking for the path back home.

"Oh, you mustn't do that," said Uncle Wiggily, as he leaned on his crutch to rest himself. "There will be time enough to eat bones after you are home. Trot along now, Peetie."

"Well, I'll just bury this bone here, where Jackie and I can get it later," said Peetie. So he dug a hole for the bone and carefully covered it with earth, where it would keep just as good as if it was in a refrigerator or an ice-box.

Well, the rabbit and the grasshopper and the puppy dog looked in all the places they could think of, and around corners and up and down the middle and on both sides, for a sight of the house of Peetie's grandpa, but they couldn't seem to find it.

And then, all of a sudden, and so quickly that it happened before you could roll a popcorn ball on top of the piano, there was a growling in the bushes, and a shaking of the leaves, and out popped a big, black bear. My! Oh, my! But he was a big, savage bear, and as soon as he saw Uncle Wiggily he cried out:

"Now I have you, my fine rabbit friend! And a puppy dog also, to say nothing of a grasshopper, with which to finish off. Oh, this is a lucky day for me!"

"You--you don't mean to say that you are going to eat us, do you?" asked Uncle Wiggily, turning pale around the ears.

"That's exactly what I do mean," said the bear in a grillery-growlery voice. "And how very lucky! It's just my dinner time," and he looked at his watch to make sure, and then shut the cover with a bang.

"Well, you can't eat me!" cried the grasshopper and with that he gave a spring and landed inside of a Jack-in-the-Pulpit growing on top of a high rock, and he pulled the cover of the plant over him so the bear couldn't see him.

"Well, the grasshopper got away," said the bear in a disappointed voice, "but I have you two yet, anyhow," and with that he made a jump, and grabbed Uncle Wiggily in one paw and Peetie Bow-Wow in the other paw. Then he hugged them tight, just like a little girl hugs, her two dollies, and the bear looked down at them, first at Uncle Wiggily and then at Peetie. And that bear showed his ugly teeth, and said in his grillery-growlery voice:

"Let me see; which one of you shall I eat first?"

Well, you can just imagine how frightened Uncle Wiggily and the puppy dog were. They didn't know what to do.

"I think I'll eat you first, Mr. Rabbit," said the bear at length, and he was just getting ready to eat Uncle Wiggily, as you would eat a strawberry, when there was a rushing sound in the bushes back of that bear, and a brave voice called out:

"No, Mr. Bear, you're not going to eat either one of them. Put Uncle Wiggily down at once and let go of Peetie Bow-Wow. At once, I say!"

"Ha! Who are you?" cried the bear, turning around quickly in order to see better. "Who are you, if I may ask?"

"I'm Jackie Bow-Wow," was the answer, "and if you don't at once do as I say I'll shoot you with my gun!"

Well, you can just imagine how surprised Uncle Wiggily and Peetie were to see Jackie standing there as brave as a lion, pointing a black gun at the black bear.

"I'm not going to let them go!" cried the bear, savagely, and he hugged the rabbit and the puppy dog tighter than ever.

"Then I'm going to shoot!" cried Jackie. "One--two--three!" he counted. "Here I go! Bang!"

"Oh, don't shoot! Don't shoot!" begged the bear, and he quickly dropped the rabbit and the doggie and then he ran away through the bushes, taking his little stubby tail with him. Then Jackie burst out laughing as hard as he could.

"What's the matter?" asked Uncle Wiggily, in surprise.

"Ha! Ha!" laughed Jackie. "What a joke on that bear! I didn't have a real gun at all. It's only a wooden one, with which I was playing hunt Indians. But he thought it was a real one, and he was so scared that he let you go. Ha! Ha! Ho! Ho!"

"It's a good thing you came along when you did," said his brother Peetie. "We were just looking for grandpa's house. I was lost, you know, and couldn't find my way back."

"I know you were and I was looking for you," spoke Jackie. Then Peetie told him about the alligator and where he had been with Uncle Wiggily, and Jackie was very glad to see his brother and the old gentleman rabbit again, and he was soon ready to show them the way to his grandpa's house.

But they had forgotten about the grasshopper in the Jack-in-the-Pulpit, and a very curious thing happened to that poor insect. I'll tell you about it on the next page, when the Bedtime Story will be named "Uncle Wiggily and the Red Monkey;" that is, if the rubber ball doesn't bounce into the rice pudding and scatter it all over the clean tablecloth.

STORY XIX
UNCLE WIGGILY AND THE MONKEY

Uncle Wiggily, with Peetie and Jackie Bow-Wow, was walking along the road toward the puppy dogs' grandpa's house, and they were talking how Jackie had made the black bear run away by pointing a make-believe wooden gun at the savage creature. All at once the old gentleman rabbit exclaimed:

"That grasshopper!"

"What about the grasshopper?" asked Jackie. "Did one bite you, Uncle Wiggily?"

"No, but my friend, the green grasshopper, jumped into a Jack-in-the-Pulpit when the bear came, and here we have come away and forgotten all about him. We must go right back."

So back they started, and on the way the rabbit told what a kind friend the grasshopper had been to him on his travels. Well, they got to the place where the bear had scared them, but when they looked up on the rock no Jack-in-the-Pulpit was to be seen, and there was no sign of the grasshopper.

"I'm sure it was here that the grasshopper made his jump," said Uncle Wiggily, looking carefully about.

"Yes," said Jackie, "but there is no Jack-in-the-Pulpit on this rock at all."

"Here is a pile of dirt, though," spoke Peetie. "Perhaps there is a bone under it. Let's dig, Jackie."

So those two puppy dogs dug in the earth while Uncle Wiggily looked all around for the grasshopper. Then, all of a sudden, Peetie cried out:

"Oh! Look here! The Jack-in-the-Pulpit is under this pile of earth! The top is just sticking out. Now, we'll find the hoppergrass."

"I see how it is," said the rabbit. "When the bear ran away so fast from Jackie's wooden gun the toenails of the savage creature

80

scattered up the earth, and it went in a shower all over the Jack where the grasshopper was hidden. No wonder we couldn't find him, for he was buried. But please dig very carefully, Peetie and Jackie, or you might scratch him with your paws."

Uncle Wiggily and the Monkey

"We will be careful," said Jackie. So he and his brother dug and dug, until the Jack-in-the-Pulpit was almost uncovered. Then they didn't dig any more, but, with their tails, which were like dusting brushes, they dashed off the earth very gently, until the plant was all clear, and out popped the grasshopper, not a bit harmed, though he was somewhat frightened.

"My! I thought I'd never get out!" exclaimed the jumping chap, taking a long breath, and blowing the dust off his legs.

Then he was introduced to Jackie Bow-Wow, whom he had not met before, and the four friends trudged along the road together. Pretty soon they came to the house of Grandpa Bark, and the old gentleman dog was very glad to see Peetie, who had been lost, and had stayed away all night.

"And I am very glad to see you also, Uncle Wiggily," said Grandpa Bark, "and likewise the grasshopper. Come in and have something to eat, and stay awhile to rest yourself."

So Uncle Wiggily did this, and after a bit he said:

"Well, now, I must be off once more to seek my fortune. When I find it I am going back home, and I hope that soon comes to pass, for I am tired of traveling about."

So he said good-by to Peetie and Jackie Bow-Wow, and he and the grasshopper hopped off together. On and on they went, over the hills and dales, through the woods and fields, and pretty soon they came to a place in the woods where there was a big box. It was almost as large as a small house, and it had a front door to it, but no windows. The front door was open and over it was a card reading:

"COME IN, IF YOU WANT TO."

"Ha, hum! I wonder if that means me?" said Uncle Wiggily. "Perhaps I may find my fortune in there. I'm going inside."

"I wouldn't if I were you," spoke the grasshopper. "It may be a trap."

"Nonsensicalness!" exclaimed the old gentleman rabbit, quick-like. "Come along. We'll go in."

So he and the grasshopper went inside, but no sooner had they entered, than slam-bang! down came the sliding door with a crash, catching them fast there just like mice in a trap.

"Oh, what did I tell you!" cried the grasshopper, sadly. "This is a trap! We're in it."

"Yes, I see we are," spoke Uncle Wiggily, much puzzled. "It was all my fault. I should have been more careful."

"Never mind," said the grasshopper, kindly, as he wiped away his tears on a piece of green leaf. "I see a crack between the boards that I can crawl through. It is too small for you, but I can get out, and I'll go for help."

So out he crawled, leaving Uncle Wiggily there. The old gentleman rabbit was thinking of the dreadful things that might happen to him, when, all of a sudden, he heard some one unlocking the front door that had fallen shut.

"I must see who that is!" whispered the rabbit to himself. So he peered out of a crack, and he saw something red and fuzzy-like at the door. "Oh, it's a red bear!" thought the rabbit, and he was looking for a place to hide, when all at once the door opened and there stood a nice, kind red monkey, with a red cap on.

"Oh, I've got company, I see!" cried the red monkey in delight. "I'm glad of that, Uncle Wiggily. I've been waiting some time to see you. How did you get here?"

"Isn't--isn't this a trap?" asked the rabbit.

"Not a bit of it!" cried the red monkey with a jolly laugh. "This is my house. I went out this morning and left the door open. It must have blown shut by mistake. I'm sorry you were frightened. Wait, I'll do some tricks to make you laugh."

So the red monkey stood on his nose, and then on one ear, and then he made all the letters of the alphabet on his tail, all except the letter "X," which is very hard for a monkey to make. Then the monkey took two apple pies and made them into one, and he and Uncle Wiggily ate it, and my! how good it was. By this time the rabbit wasn't frightened any more, and he told the red monkey all about his travels to find a fortune. And then the grasshopper came hopping back with Old Dog Percival to help Uncle Wiggily get out of the trap, but there wasn't any need, for it was no trap at all, you see.

So the red monkey and the dog and the grasshopper and the old gentleman rabbit had a nice time at the house of the red monkey, who told them many stories, and one was how he came to be colored red.

I'll tell you about that as soon as I can, when, in case the fishpole doesn't go out in the rain and catch cold, the Bedtime Story will be about Uncle Wiggily and the butterfly.

STORY XX
UNCLE WIGGILY AND THE BUTTERFLY

"You have a very nice house here," said Uncle Wiggily to the red monkey after they had all sat down, and Old Dog Percival had been told that there was no need to rescue his rabbit friend from a trap.

"Yes, it is a fine little house," said the red monkey. "I built it away off in the woods so as to be nice and quiet. You see I used to live with the monkey who plays five hand organs at once, but finally it got so that I couldn't stand the music any longer, so I went off by myself and made this little house."

"But how did you happen to get splashed with that lovely red color?" asked the grasshopper, "that is if you will excuse me asking you such a personal question."

"Pray do not mention it, I beg of you," said the red monkey as he tossed up a lump of coal and caught it on his nose. "I will gladly tell you how I became colored red. It was this way: I was writing a letter to a friend of mine and I had no more black ink left. I didn't know what to do until I happened to think that out in the yard back of my house on a bush were some red raspberries. I gathered some of them and put them in a teacup.

"Then, with the potato-masher, I crushed them all up until the red juice ran out. Then I had the loveliest red ink you ever saw. But just then a fly lit on the end of my nose. I went to brush him off with the potato-masher when I happened to hit the cup full of red juice by mistake.

"Well, you can imagine what happened. The raspberry juice splashed all over me until I looked like a strawberry ice-cream cone, and I've been red ever since."

"It's a very fine color," said Uncle Wiggily.

"Yes," agreed the monkey with a sigh "but sometimes it's quite a trouble. All the turkey gobblers and the bulls in the fields chase me whenever they see me, for they don't like red. I'm thinking of taking some dandelions and coloring myself yellow next year. But, now tell me of your travels, Uncle Wiggily."

So the old gentleman rabbit did so, mentioning how he was searching for his fortune, but couldn't find it. Then Percival told about when he used to be in a circus and do tricks, and the grasshopper told how he made his music by playing the fiddle with his left hind leg, and then the red monkey gave them all some chocolate-cocoanut pudding and it was time to go to bed.

Now, I have something sad to tell you, but please don't get alarmed, for I'll make it come out right at the end. In the middle of the night poor Uncle Wiggily was taken ill. He had a dreadful pain, and he was as hot with a fever as a stove with a fire in it.

"I am afraid you have been traveling about too much," said the red monkey, as he lighted a lamp and gave the rabbit a drink of cool water. "We must have Dr. Possum see you in the morning."

"Perhaps I ate too much chocolate-cocoanut pudding," said Uncle Wiggily. "Oh, how I suffer, and how hot I am."

Well, they did all they could for him by putting his paws in mustard water and giving him sweet spirits of nitre, but it didn't seem to do any good.

"Yes, he is a very sick rabbit," said Dr. Possum, who came in the morning. "He ought to be home in bed, but we can't move him now. He'll have to stay here."

"Oh, the grasshopper and Old Dog Percival and I will take good care of him," said the red monkey, kindly.

"Yes, I guess you will," agreed Dr. Possum. So he left some bitter medicine for Uncle Wiggily and the old gentleman rabbit took it without even wrinkling up his nose--and it was very, very bitter-- the medicine I mean, and not his nose.

"Oh, how hot I am!" cried Uncle Wiggily, as the sun got higher and higher in the sky and beat down on the house where the red monkey lived. "I wish I had some ice." Then he fell asleep.

"We will see if we can't find some," said the grasshopper, so he and the monkey and Old Dog Percival started off to look for an ice-house, leaving Uncle Wiggily asleep. Pretty soon he awakened.

"Oh, I wish I had an electric fan to cool me!" cried the poor sick old gentleman rabbit. "Oh, how hot I am! Oh, dear!"

Well, he kept getting hotter and hotter, and tossed to and fro on the bed, and he wished for ice, and ice-cream cones and all such cool things as those. Then, all of a sudden, when he was so warm he couldn't seem to stand it any longer he heard a little voice singing this song:

"Away up North in the ice and snow,
That's the place for you to go.
Where wintry winds do always blow,
And the polar bear's on a big ice floe.
"Where seals dive down in the icy sea,
Where it's far too cold for a bug like me,
Where snowflakes fall so you cannot see,
That is the place for you to be."

"Oh, I'm sure it is," cried poor Uncle Wiggily. "I wish I was up there in the Arctic regions. But I can't go. Oh, if I only had an electric fan to cool me off!"

"I'll be an electric fan for you," said the voice, and turning his head, Uncle Wiggily saw, perched on the window-sill, a beautiful big butterfly, with red and yellow wings. Then the splendid creature flew right up on the rabbit's pillow, and began to wave his wings. Faster and faster the butterfly's wings went until you couldn't see them move--just like an electric fan. And a cool breeze swept over poor, hot Uncle Wiggily, and made him feel much better.

Then the butterfly fluttered harder than ever, and he sang another song about ice-cream freezers and blizzards and snow and hail and icebergs and polar bears and all cool things like that, and he kept on fanning the rabbit with his wings, and before he knew it Uncle Wiggily went fast asleep again.

Then, in a little while, the grasshopper and the red monkey and Old Dog Percival came back with some ice and they gave the rabbit a cool drink, and the butterfly kept on fanning him. And soon Dr. Possum came in, and he said:

"Well, I do declare! Uncle Wiggily is all well again. The butterfly with his cool wings and cold songs has cured him."

Then the rabbit thanked the beautiful winged creature very kindly and got ready to go on seeking his fortune again next day. He had quite an adventure, too, and I'll tell it to you on the next page, when, in case the little boy across the street doesn't lose his mittens inside a watermelon and freeze his rubber boots, the story will be about Uncle Wiggily and roast potatoes.

STORY XXI
UNCLE WIGGILY AND THE POTATOES

"Well, how are you feeling this beautiful morning, Uncle Wiggily?" asked the red monkey, as he knocked on the door of a hollow stump where the rabbit had spent the night. "Are you all better?" the red monkey went on, as he took a cocoanut out of his pocket and looked inside the shell to see what time it was.

"Oh, yes, I am much better, thank you kindly for asking," said the rabbit. "But how comes it that you are here? I thought you were off in the woods."

"So I was," answered the monkey, as he nibbled a little bit of the cocoanut. "But I came here to keep you company and help you look for your fortune."

"Ha! But where is my friend the grasshopper?" asked Uncle Wiggily, sort of anxious-like.

"Oh, he had to hop away in the night to see a sick cousin of his," spoke the red monkey, "and on his way he jumped past my house and asked me if I wouldn't come and stay with you while he was gone. He said you might be lonesome. So I came."

"It is very kind of you, I'm sure," said the rabbit. "I like company. I think I am all well and strong again, for the butterfly, who pretended he was an electric fan, made me nice and cool and I am much better. I am ready to start off now and look once more for my fortune. Are you coming?"

"I am," said the red monkey, looking at his tail to see if a pink cow had stepped on it. But no pink cow was there, so after Uncle Wiggily had put some cherry pie in his valise he and the monkey started off together.

And, on the way, the red monkey--who was red, you know, because some red ink which he made from raspberry juice splashed on him--this red monkey, as he and Uncle Wiggily walked along, tossed the cocoanut up in the air and caught it as it came down. Sometimes the monkey would catch the cocoanut in his left paw and sometimes in his right, and again in his left foot, and still again in his right foot. So altogether he had quite an exciting time, you see.

Well, Uncle Wiggily looked on all sides for his fortune, but he couldn't seem to find it. The red monkey helped him, too, but it was of no use. On and on they went, over the hills and through the woods and across the fields, until finally they came to a place where there were a whole lot of stones made into a sort of a fireplace, as if some boys had built it to play camp, and hunt the Indians, only, of course, you know, there aren't really any Indians to hunt any more.

"Hum suz dud!" exclaimed Uncle Wiggily, as he sat down on a log, and looked at the stone fireplace, "I wonder what this is for?"

"I don't know," said the monkey, as he made the cocoanut whiz about like a merry-go-round, "I don't know what it is for, but I should say it was very lucky for us."

"Why so!" asked Uncle Wiggily, and he wiped the dust off his red-white-and-blue-barber-pole crutch on his fuzzy ears. "Why is this lucky for us?"

"Because," answered the monkey, "here are some potatoes growing in this field next door, and here is a place to make a fire. It is nearly dinner time, so there is nothing to stop us from having some roast potatoes for our lunch."

"Fine!" cried Uncle Wiggily. "I don't believe the man who owns the potatoes will mind if we take a few. I'll dig them with my paws, and we'll cook some."

"And I'll make the fire," said the red monkey as he looked about for a puddle of water. You know, he wanted the water puddle to use as a looking-glass, in order to see if any of the red had come off him yet. But there was no water, so he didn't bother, but instead he gathered the wood, and soon he had made a fine fire in the stone fireplace. Then along came Uncle Wiggily with some potatoes which he had dug, and they were put in to roast.

My! how the fire did blaze when the monkey kept putting sticks of wood on it. And how the potatoes roasted and crackled there in the heat! Oh, how nice they smelled, too! It makes me hungry for some, and as soon as I finish this story I'm going out and roast some just as Uncle Wiggily did.

But you children mustn't do it unless your papa, or mamma, or big brother or sister is near, in case any sparks got on you and burned you. But the red monkey and Uncle Wiggily were very careful. To be sure some smoke got in the monkey's eyes, and he looked as if he were crying, and some smoke got up Uncle Wiggily's twinkling nose and made him sneeze, but they didn't mind that.

"I guess the potatoes are cooked now," said the monkey after a while, and he took out on a sharp-pointed stick a big potato and broke it open. "Yes, it's done," he went on, as he saw how mealy and flaky-white the potato was, even if the outside was burned black. Then he and Uncle Wiggily took out some more of the potatoes, and when they were cool the two friends put salt on them, and ate them all up. Then the monkey played ball with his cocoanut again.

And, all of a sudden, as he threw the cocoanut quite high up in the air, it came down in the middle of a prickly briar bush. Then, all at once, there was a terrible roaring sound and a savage voice cried out from the middle of the bushes:

"Hi, there! Who is throwing stones at me?"

Then, before Uncle Wiggily or the red monkey could move, out sprang the skillery-scalery alligator with his double-jointed tail. Right at the red monkey and poor Uncle Wiggily he rushed, and he cried:

"Who threw that stone?"

"Please, Mr. Alligator," said the monkey, "it wasn't a stone. It was my cocoanut, and I didn't mean to hurt you."

"A cocoanut, eh?" roared the alligator. "So much the worse for you! I'm going to eat you both. Here I come! Get ready!"

And with that he opened his mouth as wide as a big paper bag, and fairly jumped for the red monkey.

"Oh, I'm gone, sure, this time!" cried the monkey, sadly-like.

"No, you're not!" shouted brave Uncle Wiggily. "I'll save you!" And what do you s'pose that rabbit gentleman did? Why, he just put on a pair of gloves, as quickly as a cat can wash her face on a rainy day, and he reached in the hot ashes, and he pulled out three hot, roast potatoes. Then, taking careful aim, he threw one hot potato right into the alligator's open mouth, which was as wide as two paper bags now, ready to eat the red monkey.

"Oh, wow!" cried the alligator, as he felt the hot potato slipping down his throat like a roast marshmallow candy.

"Wait, I'm not done yet," shouted the rabbit, and he threw hot potato number two down the alligator's throat.

"Wow! Wow!" cried the skillery-scalery creature as he felt the blistering heat on his forty-'leven sharp teeth.

"Wait! I have something more for you!" exclaimed Uncle Wiggily, and then with slow and careful aim, he threw hot roast potato number three down the alligator's throat.

"Wow! Wow! Wow!" yelled the skillery-scalery creature, and then, fairly boiling inside, he turned a big backward somersault, standing up on the end of his double-jointed tail, and he ran off to find some iced water with which to cool himself.

"Ha! That's the time you saved my life with the roast potatoes. They were just fine!" cried the red monkey. Then he and Uncle Wiggily traveled on, and the alligator didn't bother them any more that day, being so busy drinking iced water.

But they had another adventure soon, and I'll tell it to you a little later, when the story will be about Uncle Wiggily and Buddy Pigg--that is if the goldfish doesn't get caught in the mosquito net and tear a hole in it for the June bugs to come in and read the fly-paper.

Uncle Wiggily and the Potatoes

STORY XXII
UNCLE WIGGILY AND BUDDY PIGG

Uncle Wiggily and the red monkey were going slowly along through the woods. It was the day after the alligator had started to eat up the little red monkey, but he had to stop when the old gentleman rabbit threw hot roast potatoes down his skillery-scalery throat.

"Do you think you will find your fortune to-day?" asked the monkey, as he tossed up a stone and caught it as it came down. You see he had lost the cocoanut he used to have that time when it hit the alligator.

"Well, I can't say for sure," replied Uncle Wiggily. "I hope I may find some gold or diamonds, so I can get rich and go back home. But you can never tell what is going to happen in this world, not even whether you are going to have an ice-cream cone or not; no, indeed, and a stick of peppermint candy besides."

"I tell you what it is," said the red monkey, slow and thoughtful-like, as he scratched his stubby black nose with a piece of straw. "I don't believe you have looked in the right places for your fortune, Uncle Wiggily."

"Why, nonsensicalness!" exclaimed the old gentleman rabbit. "I look in every place I can think of. I look on the ground, and under stones, and behind stumps, and down holes, and alongside of rail fences. But I haven't found any gold or diamonds yet."

"Exactly," spoke the red monkey. "But did you ever look up a tree for them?"

"Once I did," said the rabbit. "I threw up a stone with some molasses and a string to it to get some gold. But the stone went in an owl's hole, I think. That's all the luck I ever had."

"Then I'm going to look up some more trees for you," went on the monkey. "I am a good climber, and perhaps I may have better luck. Hop along lively now and maybe we will find your fortune before breakfast."

So the two friends went along together, and every once in a while the monkey would climb a tree. The first one he scrambled up was a maple tree, and he hoped he might find some maple sugar hanging on the branches, but it wasn't time for maple sugar. Anyhow, you remember that this kind of sugar comes from the inside of a tree and not the outside. They take the tree juice and boil it in the spring of the year, you know, and that makes maple sugar.

The next tree the monkey went up was a hickory nut tree, and there were some nuts on it, but they weren't ripe yet, and when he ate one it was so bitter that he had to make a funny face. And Uncle Wiggily, who was on the ground, happened to see the monkey's funny face, and the old gentleman rabbit laughed so hard that he dropped his valise.

The valise came open and out fell a piece of cherry pie, and when the monkey saw this he laughed. He laughed so hard that he shook the tree, and a whole lot of green hickory nuts fell down, and two of them struck Uncle Wiggily on the end of his twinkling nose, making him sneeze forty-'leven times.

Then the monkey was sorry, and he scrambled to the ground without having found any gold or diamond fortunes. He said he was sorry that Uncle Wiggily was hurt.

"Pray do not mention it," spoke the rabbit, politely. "It was partly my fault. Let us hurry on."

"No, let's eat breakfast first," suggested the monkey; so they sat down and ate the cherry pie, after brushing off the dirt, and really it wasn't damaged hardly any.

Well, then they traveled on again, and the next tree which the monkey climbed was a pine tree, and on it were long pine cones, something like brown bananas, but not very good to eat. The monkey began picking them, and Uncle Wiggily called out:

"Have you found any fortune for me?"

"No," said the red monkey, sadly, "I haven't, but we can have a game of baseball with these cones when I come down. Look out, I'm going to toss some to you."

Uncle Wiggily got safely out of the way behind a big stone, and the red monkey tossed down a number of the long, brown pine cones. And just as the first of them were nearing the ground a most surprising thing happened. Out from the woods came a big black bear, and he walked toward the tree in which the monkey was, just in time to be hit on the end of his soft and tender nose by the sharp pine cones which the monkey threw.

"Wow!" cried the bear. "Who did that?"

Well, of course, Uncle Wiggily wasn't going to say that he had done it, for he hadn't, so the rabbit just crouched down behind the rock, and waited to see what would happen.

And the monkey hadn't seen the bear, so he threw down some more pine cones, and land sakes flopsy dub and a potato pancake! one of the cones hit the bear on his soft nose again!

"Wow! Wow!" cried the bear once more. "Who did that?"

And this time he happened to look up, and there he saw the poor red monkey up in the pine tree.

"Ah, ha! It's you, is it?" growled the bear. "Now, just for that I'm going to climb up there and eat you."

"Oh, please don't!" begged the monkey. "It was all a mistake. I didn't mean to do it!"

"Well, there won't be any mistake about this!" growled the bear. "Here I come!" And up he climbed, for bears can climb a tree better than can a cat.

Well, you can just imagine how scared that monkey was. He was so frightened that he didn't think to run to the top of the pine tree, and jump into another, so he could get away. Instead he just sat there on a limb, shivering. And Uncle Wiggily was also frightened as he hid behind the stone.

"The poor monkey will be eaten up," thought the rabbit, "and it will be my fault, because he was looking for my fortune. Oh! what can I do?"

And just then Uncle Wiggily heard a rustling in the leaves at his feet. He jumped back, thinking it might be a little baby bear, but, instead out pounced a tiny brown and white chap without any tail.

"Why, Buddy Pigg!" exclaimed the rabbit. "How does it happen that you are here?"

"I'm just walking about for exercise," said the guinea-pig boy, for he it was. "But what is the trouble, Uncle Wiggily?"

"The bear is going to eat up the red monkey," said the old gentleman rabbit, sadly. "Look!"

Buddy Pigg looked, and by this time the bear had almost climbed up to where the monkey was sitting and shivering.

"Oh, I must stop that!" exclaimed Buddy. "Wait a minute and watch. You know how I can whistle, don't you? so listen."

Now, you know all guinea pigs can make a funny, squeaking noise just like some one whistling, and that's exactly what Buddy did. He whistled loudly and he whistled softly through his teeth. Then he whistled double and single and next he whistled like a man calling to his dog.

And that's exactly what the bear thought it was--a man whistling for the dogs to come and bite the bear. Louder whistled Buddy through his teeth, hiding down behind the rock with Uncle Wiggily, and the bear was very much frightened.

"I guess the dogs are coming for me!" the bear exclaimed, and he stopped climbing up the tree. Then he called to the monkey: "I'll get you some other time." Then the bear slid down the tree and ran off in the woods, while Buddy whistled louder than ever. And then the monkey came safely down, and he wasn't eaten by the bear, after all, and that's all to this story, if you please.

The next one will be about Uncle Wiggily and Munchie Trot, the pony boy--that is if the automobile horn doesn't stick in the lace curtains and scare the fish cakes so that they bite the mashed potatoes.

STORY XXIII
UNCLE WIGGILY AND MUNCHIE TROT

"Weren't you frightened when you were up in the tree and the bear was coming after you?" asked Buddy Pigg of the red monkey, as he and Uncle Wiggily were walking along, after the adventure that I told you about last night.

"Frightened? I should say I was!" exclaimed the monkey. "I thought I'd never get down again to help look for Uncle Wiggily's fortune. I never can thank you enough for whistling and scaring that savage bear. How do you do it?"

"Oh, it is very simple," said the guinea pig boy, as he modestly looked down at the ground. "It's this way."

Then he whistled through his teeth again, slowly and faster, just to show how it was done.

"I wish I could learn how to do that," said the monkey. "If I ever get caught up a tree again by a bear I could whistle for myself, and make believe some hunter's dogs were coming to help me."

"I'll show you," said Buddy Pigg, and he told the monkey how to put his tongue against his teeth and how to blow through his lips. Well, the red monkey tried it, and he tried again, but he couldn't seem to whistle.

"Perhaps if I stand on my head I could do better," he said, and in a moment there he was standing on his head and trying to whistle upside down. But still he couldn't do it.

"Try hanging by your tail," suggested Buddy Pigg, and the little red chap did so, but still it was of no use. He hung there by his tail so long that Uncle Wiggily was afraid the monkey's head might fall off, so he made him get down.

Then the red chap tried again and again, but he couldn't whistle a bit, and at last the old gentleman rabbit said:

"I believe I know what the trouble is."

"What?" asked Buddy.

"Why, you see you have no tail, Buddy, and you are a good whistler," went on the rabbit, for you know it's really so--guinea pigs have no tails--though I'm not allowed to tell you the reason just yet.

"You have no tail, and you are a good whistler," said the rabbit again, "but the monkey has a long tail, and he can't seem to whistle a bit. The tail must make all the difference. Just cut off your tail, red monkey, and you'll whistle."

"Yes, I guess I would!" exclaimed the monkey, surprised-like. "I'd cry too, and feel very badly. No, if I have to lose my tail to whistle I'll never do it. I know what I can do instead."

"What?" asked Buddy Pigg.

"I can hire a green parrot to whistle for me," said the monkey. "Parrots can whistle for real or make-believe dogs as good as a man can. I'll take a parrot with me, and he'll scare the bears."

"Very good," said Uncle Wiggily, "for I would not like to see you lose your tail."

So, the three friends traveled on for some distance until it was time for Buddy Pigg to go home. And with him Uncle Wiggily sent his love to all his friends and to Sammie and Susie Littletail also.

"Well, we don't seem to be finding your fortune very fast," spoke the red monkey after they had climbed up one hill, and part of another one, and had looked under a lot of stones and behind several stumps.

"No, I guess we won't find it to-day," said the rabbit. It was now getting on toward afternoon, and Uncle Wiggily began thinking of where he would spend the night.

"I know what to do," said the red monkey. "I'll make a little house here in the woods, and we'll stay in that. We'll build a fire, and make believe we are camping out. And, while I am making the house out of sticks and leaves, you can walk around and look for your fortune."

"Very good," said the old gentleman rabbit, and so he started off, leaving the monkey to make the house in the woods. Uncle Wiggily walked on and on, but he didn't find his fortune, and it was getting rather late. He was just about to start back to where he had left the red monkey, when all of a sudden he heard a crying in the woods.

"Ha! I know what that is!" exclaimed the rabbit. "That is a baby fox, and near him is the old papa fox, who wants to catch and eat me. I'll not go near him, but I'll hurry home."

So he started toward the monkey's house, but the crying became louder, and the rabbit thought that perhaps, after all, it might not be a baby fox. And then, before he could twinkle his nose more than seven times, there was a rustling in the bushes, and out came a little boy squirrel. One of his legs was broken, and he was limping along on a piece of wood for a crutch.

"Oh, you poor little fellow!" cried the rabbit. "You look just like Billie or Johnny Bushytail after a football game. What has happened?"

"Oh, a boy threw a stone at me, and hurt me!" answered the little squirrel. "I'm lost and I can't walk home, and I don't know what to do."

"I'll help you," spoke Uncle Wiggily, kindly, but when he tried to, he found that his own rheumatism was so bad that he could hardly move. And the little boy squirrel was so stiff that he could barely walk, and there they were, both in the woods, with night coming on, and no way to get home.

"Oh, what shall we do?" cried Uncle Wiggily, and he wished the monkey would come along. And just then, if you will believe me, there was another rustling in the bushes, and out galloped Munchie Trot, the strong pony boy.

"Ha! What is the trouble here?" he asked, switching his tail, just like a wooden horse on the merry-go-round.

"Oh, we are both so lame that we can't walk," said Uncle Wiggily, "and we are a long way from the monkey's house. What shall we do?"

"Yes!" cried the little lame squirrel boy, "Boo-hoo! Hoo-boo what shall we do?"

"Don't say another word!" cried Munchie. "I'll take care of you. Just get on my back and I'll soon take you to the monkey's house in the woods." Then the pony boy knelt down so that Uncle Wiggily and the squirrel could get up on his back.

And when they got there and the cupboard was bare--oh, please excuse me, that belongs in another story--when they got up on Munchie's back and were holding tightly to the saddle, off the pony boy started through the woods, galloping to the monkey's house.

Then a whole lot of mosquitoes swarmed out of the bushes and tried to bite Uncle Wiggily and the squirrel, but Munchie switched his tail at the stinging insects, and away they scattered.

Then a big owl flew down out of a tree and tried to grab the squirrel, but the pony trotted so fast that the owl was left behind. And next a wolf tried to pull the rabbit off the horse, but Munchie tickled the savage creature in the ribs with his hoof, and the wolf ran away, sneezing.

Then the pony came safely to the house that the monkey had built in the woods, and he and Uncle Wiggily and the squirrel stayed there in peace and quietness all night, and they put some salve and a bandage on the squirrel's hurt leg to make it well.

And the next day there was another adventure. I'll tell you what it was on the next page, when the story will be about Uncle Wiggily and the green parrot--that is, if the piano key doesn't unlock the front door and let in a red, white and blue mosquito to bite the baby's toes.

STORY XXIV
UNCLE WIGGILY AND THE PARROT

Uncle Wiggily was the first one to awaken in the little house that the monkey had built in the woods. It was the morning after the day when Munchie Trot had brought the rabbit and the little squirrel boy home on his back.

"Well, my rheumatism is somewhat better to-day," said the old gentleman rabbit to himself as he stretched out first one leg and then the other to see if they hurt him. He didn't have much pain, so he started to make the fire to boil the coffee.

And some of the wood which he put on the fire was wet so that it smoked. And the smoke got up the monkey's nose, and made him sneeze, so that he was awakened, and he helped to get the breakfast in a hurry.

Then, in turn, Munchie Trot woke up, and next the squirrel boy. His leg hurt him very much, but Uncle Wiggily and the monkey bound it up with some splints, and some soft bark, tying it with ribbon grass, and then they all had breakfast, and felt better.

"But how am I to get home?" asked the little squirrel boy. "My mamma and papa will worry about me, I know."

"Oh, as to that," said Munchie Trot, switching his long tail to keep the flies off the breakfast table, "I will take you home on my back."

"Very good," said Uncle Wiggily, "and I will go a little way with you, and come back here. Perhaps I may find part of my fortune in that way."

"That's nice," spoke the red monkey, "and I'll stay here and get dinner. And, say, Uncle Wiggily, if you happen to see a green parrot just bring him along to whistle for me."

"I will," promised the old gentleman rabbit. Then he helped the little lame squirrel boy up on the pony's back, and off Munchie started with Uncle Wiggily hopping alongside. The rabbit looked for his fortune, but he couldn't find it, and pretty soon he had come as far as he thought he ought to go, so he said he would start back.

"Good-by," called the lame squirrel boy, "and thank you so much for being kind to me. Perhaps you may find your fortune on your way back."

"Or, if you don't find that," spoke Munchie, as he waved good-by with his long tail, "perhaps you will find the green parrot."

Then Uncle Wiggily hopped back toward where he had left the monkey getting dinner at the little house in the woods. And, just as the old gentleman rabbit was passing under a butternut tree, he heard a voice singing this little song:

"Oh, I'm a jolly, jolly sailor lad,
I sail the ocean blue.
And if you're glad, and not very bad,
I'd like to sail with you.
Oh, it's yo-ho-ho when the wind does blow,
And the waves run mountains high.
We will skip along and sing a song
Beneath the bright blue sky.
"Oh, once I lived in a big wire cage,
In a house upon a hill.
For birds like me were the style you see,
Though I sometimes felt quite ill.
I had seeds to eat, in a seed dish neat,
But they didn't agree with me,
So I flew away on a rainy day,
To live in a greenwood tree."

"My, that's rather strange," said Uncle Wiggily. "I don't see how a sailor lad could live in a cage, nor yet perch in a tree. I must look into this. Perhaps it may be the beginning of my fortune."

So he crept along very softly, and there, perched on the limb of a tree, was a nice green parrot, scratching his crooked beak with his left foot.

"Ha! How do you do? How are the oysters? Have you been in swimming? Pass the crackers, please. Right this way for your hot ice-cream cones!" quickly cried the green parrot in a shrill voice.

"Well of all things!" exclaimed the rabbit. "I am pretty well, thank you, but I don't know anything about oysters, and I haven't been in swimming. I don't see any crackers to pass, and, as for hot ice-cream cones, I never heard of them."

"Ha! Ha!" laughed the parrot. "Never mind me. That was only my joking way. But I'm glad to see you anyhow. I was only fooling about hot ice-cream cones. Listen and I'll whistle a song for you," and then and there, without even wiggling his tail once, he whistled a song called: "Never Drop a Penny Down a Crack in the Boardwalk."

"How do you like that?" asked the parrot as he stood on one leg and stretched out his wings.

"It was very fine," said the rabbit. "And I believe you are just what I am looking for. Will you kindly come and whistle for the monkey, so the bears won't catch him?"

"I certainly will," spoke the parrot, politely. "Show me the way. I am very fond of monkeys. I used to know one who could play five hand organs at once--one with his tail."

"This is a red monkey, and he is a friend of the hand organ one," said Uncle Wiggily, as he hopped on ahead to show the green parrot the way.

Well, pretty soon, not so very long, they came near to the place where the little house was. They heard a curious hissing noise, like a steam radiator sissing in cold weather.

"My! What's that? A snake?" asked the parrot, in alarm. Uncle Wiggily looked through the bushes. Then he laughed.

"It is only the monkey trying to whistle," said the rabbit, "but he can't do it."

"Poor fellow!" spoke the green parrot kindly. "I'll whistle for him," and he did so. At first the monkey was frightened, thinking some real dogs were coming at the sound of the whistle, but then Uncle

Wiggily and the parrot popped out of the bushes, laughing, and they told the monkey who they were, the rabbit explaining that the parrot had come to whistle and scare the bears away.

"It's very kind of you," said the red monkey, "and perhaps in time I may learn to whistle a little myself. But come now and have dinner."

So the monkey and the parrot and Uncle Wiggily ate their lunch and in the afternoon they all looked for the old gentleman's fortune, but they couldn't find it. And that night something very strange happened as they were all sleeping in the little house which the monkey had built in the woods.

It was all dark and quiet when, all of a sudden, the fuzzy fox sneaked up. He broke open the front window, and he was just crawling in through the hole to eat up the rabbit when the parrot was quickly awakened by feeling the wind blowing on him through the broken glass. Then he saw the burglar fox, and he whistled for the make-believe dogs and cried out:

"Fire! Thieves! Police! Bean-soup! Trolley Cars! Ice-cream cones! Robbers! Get out of here! Take your tail with you! Police! Mud pies! Cocoanut pudding! Merry-go-rounds! Look out! Fire! Fish hooks! Automobiles! Bang-bang! Whoop-de-doodle-do!"

Well, if you'll believe me, that fuzzy fox was never so frightened in all his life before. He thought a whole lot of soldiers, and guns, and dogs, and police were after him, and he jumped out of the window and ran off as fast as his legs would take him. Then Uncle Wiggily and the green parrot and the red monkey went to sleep again, and there's no more to this story, as you can see for yourself.

But in case the umbrella doesn't turn outside in, and scare the spoon holder off the table and make the napkins jump over the sugar bowl, the next story will be about Uncle Wiggily and the hippity-hop toad.

STORY XXV
UNCLE WIGGILY AND THE HOPTOAD

"Dear me!" exclaimed Uncle Wiggily as he got out of bed the morning after the green parrot had scared away the fuzzy fox, "I do seem to be having the most surprising adventures, but I can't find my fortune. Anyhow, I'm glad we had the parrot with us last night; aren't you, red monkey?"

"Indeed I am," declared the little chap with the long tail. "And perhaps he will bring us good luck, and you may come across your fortune at any moment. Why don't you go look for it while I take my whistling lesson?"

"Are you going to try again to whistle?" asked the rabbit.

"Indeed I am," replied the monkey. "I'm not going to give up just because I can't do a thing the first time or the forty-'leventh time. If it's possible for me to whistle I'm going to learn."

"Bravo!" cried the parrot, fluttering his green wings. "That's the way to talk. Well, now we'll have breakfast, and after that I'll give you a whistling lesson, but first I must sing a song." So he sang this one:

"Once there was a dollie,
Who could shut her eyes,
They were blue like buttercups,
Under summer skies.
She had hair like roses,
And her teeth were red,
Sometimes when she walked along
She stood on her head.
"Inside her was sawdust,
Fine as fine could be,
Made from sawing little boards
That grew in a tree.
She could walk on tiptoes,
Also skip a rope,

107

Every Sunday morning she
Washed her face with soap."

"My! That was a funny doll, with red teeth and hair like roses," said the monkey. "I wonder if she was any relation to me?"

"And who ever heard of blue buttercups?" asked the rabbit. "Buttercups are yellow! Every one knows that."

"I know," said the parrot. "You see there really wasn't ever any such dollie--I just made up that song as I went along. But now for breakfast. Yo, ho! Ho, yo!"

Well, it was a nice breakfast they all had together in the little house the monkey had built, and when it was over the parrot started on the whistling lesson. Uncle Wiggily watched the monkey for a time, and saw the long-tailed chap turn a double back somersault when he found he couldn't whistle any other way. But even that didn't seem to do any good.

"Never mind," said the parrot, kindly; "you may learn yet. Never give up!"

"I'll not," said the monkey.

"Well, I think I will go off and see if I can find my fortune," said Uncle Wiggily. "I'll come back to dinner," and off he hopped, looking on all sides for gold or diamonds so that he could get rich and go back home to live in peace and comfort.

Well, the old gentleman rabbit hadn't gone on very far before he came to a place where there was a hole in the ground, and in front of it was a sign, which read:

"HOP DOWN HERE AND GET
RICH."

"Ah, ha!" exclaimed the rabbit. "Indeed, I'll not do that. There must be a bad fox or a bear down there. I'll keep away." So he hopped on very quickly, and a voice called out after him:

"Aren't you coming down and get rich?"

"No, I'm not!" answered the rabbit, as he looked back and saw a savage mud turtle sticking his long neck and snaky head out of

108

the hole. Then the rabbit kept on, and he went so fast that the turtle couldn't catch up to him.

Well, the next place he came to was a little pond of water, and in front of this was a piece of paper on which was written:

"JUMP IN HERE AND GET RICH."

"Ah, ha! No, indeed!" exclaimed Uncle Wiggily, foxy-like. "They can't catch me that way! There is probably an alligator in that pond."

So away he ran as fast as he could go, and a voice cried after him:

"Aren't you coming in?" And, looking back, he saw a big, savage water rat.

"No, indeed; I'm not coming in," said the old gentleman rabbit, and he hurried on, while the water rat gnashed his sharp teeth, because he was so disappointed at not catching the rabbit.

Well, the next place Uncle Wiggily came to was a big, bright, tin can standing beside the path that led through the woods.

"Ha! I wonder what that can be?" thought the rabbit. "Perhaps there is a sign on it telling me to climb in and get rich." So he looked all around the tin can, but there was no sign. "That must be a safe place," thought the rabbit. "It may be full of gold or diamonds. I'm going to have a look in."

He tried to climb up the sides of the can, but they were too smooth, so he got some long sticks and some short ones, and, by tying them together with ribbon grass, Uncle Wiggily made a little ladder. Then, by standing this up against the tin can, he could climb up and look in.

When he first looked over the top of the can he couldn't see anything. Then he leaned away far over, and the first thing he knew, in he had fallen ker-splash! and the can was full of molasses--yes, there poor Uncle Wiggily was in a can of molasses and he was so stuck up that he didn't know what to do.

He tried to swim out, but the molasses was too thick. And he kept sinking deeper and deeper.

"Oh, dear! What shall I do?" he cried. "I can never get out!"

And then, all of a sudden, a voice outside the can called:

"Who are you, and what is the trouble?"

"Oh, please help me," begged the rabbit.

"I will," said the voice again. "I am the hippity-hop toad, and I am going to take that can up on my back, and hippity-hop up and down with it until I turn all the molasses into molasses candy, and then you can climb out on that. Hold fast, please."

Well, Uncle Wiggily held fast, and the first thing he knew the can in which he was a prisoner gave a lurch and a swaying motion, and then it almost turned upside down, and then he knew it must be up on the back of the hippity-hop toad.

Then, my goodness! I wish you could have seen that toad hop. Up and down he went like the dasher in a churn, or like a steam pump. Up and down! Up and down, faster and faster! The molasses splashed all over and some got up Uncle Wiggily's nose and some in his eyes, and it was all he could do to hold on to the sides of the can. But somehow he managed it.

But pretty soon the molasses got thicker and thicker, and then it began to get harder and harder, and pretty soon it was turned into sticks of molasses candy. Then Uncle Wiggily took these candy sticks and made a ladder of them, and when the hippity-hop toad set down the can off his back the rabbit climbed up the inside of it on his candy ladder, went down his wooden ladder outside the can and he was safe.

Of course he had lots of spots of molasses on him, but the toad showed him where there was a brook of water in which he washed himself. Then he thanked the hippity-hop toad and went back to the monkey house, though still without his fortune.

Now in the next story, in case the mucilage bottle doesn't upset on the doormat and make the letterman stick fast to it so he can't whistle, I'll tell you about Uncle Wiggily and the angle worms.

STORY XXVI
UNCLE WIGGILY AND THE WORMS

"Well, where in the world have you been?" asked the red monkey of Uncle Wiggily, as the old gentleman rabbit hopped along after he had gotten out of the molasses can.

"Oh, I had an adventure," replied the rabbit, and he told how the hippity-hop toad had saved him from the sticky stuff. "But can you whistle yet, red monkey?" asked Uncle Wiggily.

"No, he doesn't seem to be able to do it," spoke the green parrot, in a sort of sad and hopeless tone. "Every time he tries to whistle he puckers his face up in such a funny way that I have to laugh, and when I laugh I can't whistle. Can't you keep your face straight, so I won't have to giggle?" asked the green bird, solemn-like.

"I can't seem to," replied the monkey, and he made another effort to whistle, but he puckered up such a funny face, and his tail got all tied up in a hard knot, and he looked so queer that even Uncle Wiggily had to laugh.

"You see how it is," said the parrot. "I can't give whistling lessons and laugh at the same time," and then he had to laugh "Ha! Ha!" and "Ho! Ho!" because you see the monkey made another queer face trying to get the knots out of his tail.

"I think I have a plan," said Uncle Wiggily after a bit.

"What is it?" asked the monkey.

"You must get behind a tree, red monkey," said the rabbit. "Then the parrot can tell you how to whistle, and give you a lesson without seeing the funny faces you make. Then he can whistle, to show you how, and he won't have to laugh."

"The very thing!" cried the parrot. So they tried that way, and they got along quite nicely. Well, by that time it was the dinner hour, and, after the meal, Uncle Wiggily said he would go out again to look for his fortune, and would come back to supper.

111

"But don't fall into any more molasses cans," cautioned the monkey, and the rabbit gentleman said he would not. Away Uncle Wiggily hopped over the hills, across the fields and through the woods. Pretty soon he came to a pile of nice brown dirt.

Uncle Wiggily and the Alligator

"Ha, some one has been digging here," thought the rabbit. "Perhaps some one else is also looking for a fortune of gold or diamonds. If that is so I had better dig here, too."

So, with his sharp paws, the rabbit began to dig in the dirt near the pile of earth. Faster and faster he dug until, all of a sudden, he saw something moving in the hole he had made.

"Ha! I wonder if there is moving-gold here?" he thought.

But when he looked again he saw that it was only a little angleworm, or earth worm, as some people call them, who was crawling out to sun himself.

"Oh, I hope I haven't hurt you!" exclaimed Uncle Wiggily, kindly, as he lifted up the worm gently in his paws.

"Not a bit of it," answered the worm, twisting about to see if his tail was all there. "But I'm glad you're not a fisherman, Mr. Rabbit."

"Why so?" asked Uncle Wiggily, as he shook some dirt out of his left ear.

"Because if you were you might stick me on a sharp hook and toss me into the water for the fish to eat. Nothing is worse than to have a hook stuck into you," said the worm, moving around until he was in two knots. Then he untied himself again.

"I should think hooks might be unpleasant," spoke the rabbit. "But I won't hurt you, and here is a bit of cherry pie for you."

"Thank you, most kindly," said the angle worm, as he sat up on the end of his tail and ate the cherry pie, juice and all. "But why are you digging in the earth, Uncle Wiggily?"

"To find my fortune," answered the rabbit, and he told how long he had been looking for gold or diamonds and how he hadn't found any yet. "Is there any gold down under the ground where you live?" asked the rabbit, sad-like.

"Not a bit, I'm sorry to say," answered the worm. "I live down there with numbers of my friends, but there is no gold. You had better dig somewhere else. But you have been very kind to me, and if ever I can do you a favor I will."

"Thank you," said Uncle Wiggily, so he hopped out of the hole he had made, and, after saying good-bye to the worm, he traveled on to find another place where he might dig for his fortune.

He came to a place in the woods, where the ground was nice and soft, and there he started to make another hole. Well, he hadn't gone down very far before, all of a sudden, he heard a growling voice behind him calling out:

"Here! Who said you could dig in my land?"

"Oh, I beg your pardon. Is this your land?" asked the rabbit, and he looked up to see the skillery-scalery alligator glaring down at him.

"Yes, this is my land, and these are my woods, and because you were so bold as to dig here I'm going to eat you up!" shouted the 'gator, lashing his double-jointed tail around in the dried leaves. "Here I come!" he cried.

Then he made a dive, with his big, wide-open jaws, down into the hole Uncle Wiggily had dug, but the rabbit didn't wait for him. Out he jumped, and away he hopped, and the 'gator crawled after him. Faster and faster ran the rabbit, and faster and faster came the alligator.

"Oh, I know he'll catch me!" thought poor Uncle Wiggily. "Oh, help! Will no one help me?" he cried.

"Yes, we'll help you!" called a little voice on the ground, and, looking down the rabbit saw the angle worm. And, crawling along with him were about a million other worms, some larger and some smaller than he. "Run along as fast as you can," said the first angle worm, "and we'll twine ourselves in knots around the alligator's legs so that he can't chase you any more. Run! Run!"

Well, you may be sure Uncle Wiggily ran as hard as he could.

"I'll get you!" cried the alligator, and he made a jump after the rabbit, but it was the last jump the skillery-scalery creature made that day. For the next instant those million angle worms just tied themselves in hard knots, and sailor knots, and bow knots, and double knots, and true lovers' knots and all sorts of knots around the tail and legs of the alligator, and he couldn't move another inch.

"Now's your chance! Hop away, Uncle Wiggily!" cried the first worm. "We'll hold the alligator here because you were so kind to me."

And the rabbit hopped safely away, and the ugly 'gator couldn't even wiggle his double-jointed tail. Then, when the rabbit was safe at the monkey's house, all the angle worms untied their knots off the alligator, and they scurried down into the ground before he could bite them. So that's how it all happened, just as true as I'm telling you. And that 'gator was so angry that he almost bit a piece out of his own tail. Then he went off in the woods and wasn't seen again for some time.

But this wasn't the last of Uncle Wiggily's adventures; no, indeed. In case the fish-hook doesn't catch the baseball and make the lamp chimney all smoky, I'll tell you next about Uncle Wiggily and the black beetle.

STORY XXVII
UNCLE WIGGILY AND THE BEETLE

One beautiful sunshiny day, when the wind was blowing through the tree-tops, making music like a church organ many miles away, Uncle Wiggily awakened in the little house which the red monkey had built for him in the deep woods.

"Well, I'm going to make another search for my fortune this morning," he said as he wiggled his whiskers to get the dried leaves out of them, for he had slept on a bed of leaves, you know.

"And I'll go with you," said the red monkey; "Because the last two or three times you went off by yourself you got into trouble."

"Trouble? I should say I did!" exclaimed the old gentleman rabbit.

"There was the time when you fell into the can of molasses, and the hippity-hop toad had to jump up and down with it on his back, until it was made into sticks of candy," said the red monkey.

"True enough," spoke Uncle Wiggily.

"And then there was the time when the skillery-scalery alligator chased you," went on the red monkey, "and the angle worms tied themselves into knots about his legs to stop him. Do you remember that?"

"Indeed I do," said the old gentleman rabbit. "And I will be very glad to have you come along with me and help me. We will start right after breakfast."

So the two friends built a little camp-fire in front of the wooden house in the woods and they cooked some oatmeal and some carrots and turnips, and Uncle Wiggily made a cherry pie with plenty of red juice in it. And the monkey found a bag of peanuts under a chestnut tree and he roasted them for his breakfast. Then they started off.

On and on they went through the woods, over the hills, up one side and down the other, around the corner, where a big gray

116

rock rested on some green moss, and then, all of a sudden, there was a queer noise up in the air. It was like wings fluttering and a voice calling. And the voice said:

"Is the red monkey down there?"

"Oh, my! I wonder who can want you?" said Uncle Wiggily.

"Maybe it's the bear who once climbed up a tree after me," cried the red monkey. "I'm going to hide." So he crawled under a big, broad leaf. Then once more the voice called:

"I want the red monkey!"

"Oh, please Uncle Wiggily, don't let him get me!" begged the shivering and shaking monkey. "Throw a stone at that bear, will you?"

"Ha! Hum!" exclaimed the old gentleman rabbit. "I don't very well see how it can be a bear. Bears don't fly in the air, for they have no wings. I'll take a look."

So he looked up in the air, and there, instead of a bear flying overhead, it was only Dickie Chip-Chip, the little sparrow boy.

"Well, bless me!" cried Uncle Wiggily. "What are you doing up there, Dickie?"

"Oh, I'm making believe I'm a messenger boy," said the sparrow. "I have a telegram for the red monkey."

"Oh, ho! So that's why you wanted me, is it?" asked the long-tailed chap, as he crawled out from under the leaf. "What is the message about, if you please?"

"Here it is," spoke Dickie, and then from under his wing he took a piece of white cocoanut with writing on it. And no sooner had the red monkey read it than he began to cry.

"What's the matter?" asked Uncle Wiggily.

"Oh, dear!" sobbed the red monkey, "my little brother who works on a hand organ nearly had his tail cut off by getting it twisted around the handle. He is very sick, and I must go home right away. Oh, how sorry I am!" and then the red monkey ate up the piece of cocoanut that had the message written on it.

117

"You had better go home at once," said Uncle Wiggily.

"But I don't like to leave you," said the red monkey.

"Oh, I will get along all right!" spoke the brave old rabbit gentleman. "Go ahead, and when your brother is well, come back."

"I will," promised the red monkey, as he started for home.

"And I'll fly on ahead to tell them he is coming," said Dickie Chip-Chip. So they both called good-by to Uncle Wiggily, and hurried away through the woods, while the rabbit gentleman kept on in search of his fortune. And now for the black beetle.

Uncle Wiggily was walking along under a green tree, looking for some gold or diamonds when, all of a sudden something jumped out of the bushes and grabbed his crutch away from him. Then Uncle Wiggily saw that it was a wolf, and the wolf sprang down into a big hole in the ground, taking the crutch with him.

"Now," called the wolf, showing his ugly teeth, "if you want your crutch, Mr. Rabbit, you'll have to come down this hole after it. Come on down."

But Uncle Wiggily knew better than that, for just as surely as he jumped down into that hole the wolf would have eaten him all up. And the rabbit didn't know what to do, for he couldn't walk without his crutch on account of being lame with the rheumatism.

"Oh, this is terrible!" cried the rabbit. "Whatever shall I do? I can't stay in these woods forever."

And just then there was a rustling in the leaves, and out walked a big black, pinching beetle. In front of his head he had two things just like fire tongs, or a crab's claws, with which to pinch.

"What is the trouble?" asked the black beetle politely.

"The wolf, down the hole, has my crutch, and he won't give it to me," said the rabbit.

"Ha! we will very soon fix that," spoke the beetle. "Just tie a string around me, Uncle Wiggily, and lower me down into the hole.

Then I'll pick up the crutch in my strong pincers, and you can haul me up again as I hold fast to it."

"But the wolf may get you," said the rabbit.

"I'll fix that wolf," replied the beetle, winking his two little eyes, real jolly-like.

So Uncle Wiggily tied a string around the black insect, and lowered him down into the hole. The wolf saw him coming and cried out:

"Oh! You can't get this crutch, for I'm sitting on it, and I'll bite you."

"Just you watch," spoke the black beetle, winking one eye this time. So he looked down, and, surely enough, the wolf was sitting on the crutch. But the beetle knew a good trick. He swung himself around on the end of the string, which the rabbit held, and, as he got near to the wolf, the beetle suddenly pinched the savage creature on the tail.

"Oh, my! Ouch!" cried the wolf, and he jumped up in a hurry. And that was just what the beetle wanted, for now he could reach the crutch as the wolf was not sitting on it any more. In his strong pincers he took hold of it.

"Pull me up!" called the beetle to the rabbit, and Uncle Wiggily did so, crutch and all, by the string, and they left the wolf down in the hole as angry as a mud pie. So that's how the beetle got back the rabbit's crutch for him, and that's the end of this story.

But there'll be another one soon, about Uncle Wiggily and Kittie Kat--that is if the puppy dog across the street doesn't chew a hole in the milk bottle and scare the iceman all to pieces so that he goes roller skating with the jumping rope.

STORY XXVIII
UNCLE WIGGILY AND KITTIE KAT

"Well," said Uncle Wiggily, as he and the black beetle went along through the woods, after the rabbit's crutch had been taken away from the savage wolf, "don't you want to come along with me, Mr. Beetle, and help me look for my fortune?"

"Indeed, I would like to very much," said the funny little insect, "but the truth of the matter is that I have to go to work to-morrow, and so I can't come."

"Work--what work do you do?" inquired Uncle Wiggily.

"Oh, I am going to punch holes in trolley car transfers with my strong pincers," answered the beetle. "Now, I will have to bid you good-by, but if ever any one takes your crutch down a hole again, send for me and I'll get it back for you."

So the beetle said good-by to the old gentleman rabbit, and went his way, and Uncle Wiggily, after looking at his crutch to be sure the wolf had not bitten a piece out of it, went on looking for his fortune.

"My! It's quite lonesome going by yourself," said the rabbit, as he hopped along through the woods. "I miss the red monkey and the grasshopper and the black beetle. But then they can't always be with me, so I'll have to travel on alone."

On and on he went. Sometimes in the fields he stopped to hear the birds sing, and he heard them talking among themselves about how they must soon get ready to go down South, for cold weather was coming. That made the old gentleman rabbit feel a little sad, and he wished that he could soon go back home, where Sammie and Susie Littletail were waiting for him.

"But I can't go until I find my fortune," he said. "I must look harder than ever for it."

Then, sometimes, when he went through the woods, he heard the little brooks whispering to the ferns, how that soon there would be ice and snow all over, with boys and girls skating and sliding down hill.

"Burr-r-r-r-r! That makes me shiver!" exclaimed the rabbit. "I, too, must get ready for winter. Oh, if I could only find that gold and those diamonds I'd go right straight home, and never travel about any more."

So he looked under stones and down in hollow stumps, but not a piece of gold nor a sparkling diamond could he find. Then it began to get late, and the sun was darkened behind the clouds.

"I wonder where I can stay to-night?" thought Uncle Wiggily. "I must pick out a nice, big stump, fill it with leaves, and sleep in there."

Well, it didn't take him long to find what he wanted, and he prepared his bed for the night. Then he built a little fire in front of the stump and cooked his supper. He ate some carrots and a turnip sandwich with peanut butter on it, and the last thing he ate was a large piece of cherry pie. Then he washed the dishes and, curling up on the soft leaves, he was soon asleep, dreaming of his little nephew and niece, Sammie and Susie.

Now, about midnight, the savage alligator, who hadn't had anything to eat in a long time, started out to find something. And pretty soon he came to the stump where Uncle Wiggily was sleeping.

"Ah, there is a good meal for me!" cried the skillery-scalery creature, as he reared up on the end of his double-jointed tail and put his long nose down in the hollow stump.

"Hey! What's this? Who is it? Has the red monkey come back?" cried the rabbit, suddenly awakening. "I'm glad to see you, Mr. Monkey. Here is some cherry pie for you."

And then, being only half awake, Uncle Wiggily took a large piece of the pie and held it out, thinking he was giving it to the monkey. But it slipped from his hand and it fell right into the alligator's face.

And the cherry juice ran down into the eyes of the skillery-scalery creature, and tickled him so that he sneezed, and then he ran away, for he thought the red monkey might possibly be in the stump, and the alligator was afraid the monkey might throw hot potatoes down his throat.

Uncle Wiggily looked out of the stump, and by the light of the silvery moon he saw the alligator running away, and that was the first time he knew it was the skillery creature, and not the monkey, who had come in so suddenly.

"My! That was a narrow escape!" cried the rabbit. "It's a good thing I took that cherry pie to bed with me. I must be on the watch, for the alligator may come back." But the skillery-scalery creature, with the double-jointed tail, didn't return, though Uncle Wiggily didn't sleep very good the rest of the night on account of being so anxious and worrying so much.

And in the morning when he awakened from a little nap the old gentleman rabbit felt very strange. He tried to get up, but he found that he couldn't. He was as dizzy as if he had been on a merry-go-round and he felt very ill.

"It must have been the fright the alligator gave me," he thought. "Oh, dear, what shall I do? Here I am, all alone in this stump in the woods, and no one to help me. Oh, I'm a poor, forsaken old rabbit, and nobody loves me! Oh, if Sammie or Susie were only here. I'm sure----"

And just then there was a scratching sound outside the stump.

"Hark! What's that?" whispered the rabbit. "That must be the alligator coming back to get me! And I can't even get up to throw some cherry pie at him. Oh, if the red monkey or the black beetle would only come!"

Then the scratching noise sounded some more, and Uncle Wiggily was getting so frightened that he didn't know what to do. And then, all of a sudden, he saw something white at the top hole of the stump, and a voice exclaimed:

"Well, if there isn't my dear old Uncle Wiggily! And you are ill, I know you are. I can tell by the way your nose twinkles."

"Indeed, I am ill," said the poor rabbit, "but who are you?" For you know he couldn't see well, as his glasses had fallen off.

"Oh, I am Kittie Kat," said the voice, and there, surely enough, was the little pussy girl. She had been away on her summer vacation, and was just coming back to get ready for school when she happened to walk through the woods. There she heard a voice in the stump, and, going to look, she saw Uncle Wiggily.

"Oh, how glad I am to see you, Kittie Kat," said the rabbit.

"And how sorry I am to see you ill," said the pussy girl. "But don't worry. I'm going to make you well. Just keep quiet."

Then that brave little pussy girl scurried around, and gathered some leaves from a plant called catnip.

"For," said Kittie, "if catnip is good for cats, it must be good for rabbits." So she made some hot catnip tea, and gave it to Uncle Wiggily, and in an hour he was all better and could sit up. Then Kittie made him some toast with some slices of yellow carrots on it, and he felt better still, and by noon he was as good as ever.

"But I don't know what I would have done, only for you, Kittie Kat," said the rabbit. "Thank you, very much. Now I can travel on and seek my fortune."

"And I'll come with you," spoke Kittie Kat. So they traveled on together, and they had an adventure the next day. I'll tell you about it right away, for the next story will be of Uncle Wiggily and Jennie Chipmunk--that is, if the green trunk up in the attic doesn't go off on a vacation all by itself down to Asbury Grove, and hide in the sand to scare the popcorn man.

STORY XXIX
UNCLE WIGGILY AND JENNIE

"Now, Uncle Wiggily," said Kittie Kat, as she and the old gentleman rabbit went along, the day after he had been cured by the catnip tea, "you must take good care of yourself. Keep in the shade, and walk slowly, for I don't want you to get sick again."

"And I don't want to myself," spoke Uncle Wiggily, "for I want to find my fortune."

"Oh, I think you will, and very soon," said Kittie. "I dreamed last night of a pile of gold and diamonds, and I'm sure you will soon be rich, so that you can come back home, and live with us all again."

"Where was the pile of gold of which you dreamed?" asked the rabbit. "Was it at the end of the rainbow? Because, if it was, there is no use to think of it. I once looked there and found nothing."

"No, it wasn't there," said Kittie, shaking her head. "I don't know where it was because I awakened before my dream was over, but I'm sure you will soon find your fortune. Now remember to walk slowly, and keep in the shade."

So she and Uncle Wiggily traveled on and on. Once they came to a big hill, which they could hardly climb, and they didn't know what to do. But they happened to meet a friendly mud turtle, who was very strong, and who had a large, broad shell.

"Get on my back," said the turtle, "and I will take you up the hill. I go slowly, but I am very sure. You will have time to rest yourselves while I am climbing up."

So Uncle Wiggily and Kittie Kat got on the turtle's back, and in time he took them up the hill. Then, after traveling on a little farther, they came to a broad river.

"Oh, how shall we ever get across?" asked Kittie.

"Perhaps I can make a boat," said the rabbit. He was looking for some wood and some broad leaves with which to make a sail, when along came swimming a big goldfish.

"Just perch upon my back," the fish said, "and I will be very glad to take you across."

"But you swim under water, and we will get all wet," objected Uncle Wiggily.

"No, I will swim with my back away up out of water," said the goldfish, and this he did, so that the rabbit and the pussy girl were taken safely over to the other side of the river and they never even so much as wet their eyelashes.

"Perhaps I may find my fortune over here," spoke Uncle Wiggily, as he hopped along after thanking the goldfish. He looked on the ground, and up in the air, but no fortune could he find.

"There is a little house, made of leaves and bark over there," said Kittie, pointing through the woods, "let us go and see who is in it."

"Perhaps a bear lives there," said the rabbit.

"It is too small for a bear's house," decided Kittie.

But as they came close to it they heard a scratching noise inside, and they thought perhaps it might be the fuzzy fox. And then, all of a sudden, they heard a voice singing this song:

"I sweep, I sew, I dust, I mend,
From morning until night.
And then I wash the plates and cups.
And scrub the table white.
"I love to make a pudding,
Also a pie and cake.
And when I do my ironing,
Potatoes do I bake.
"Now I must hurry--hurry,
To get a meal for you,
And then I'll go and gather
A hickory nut or two."

"Why, I know who that is!" cried Kittie Kat.

"Who?" asked Uncle Wiggily, making his nose twinkle like three stars and a moon on a frosty night.

"It's Jennie Chipmunk!" cried Kittie. "I just know it is. Oh, Jennie!" she called. "Is that you?"

"Yes, who is it that wants me?" asked a voice, and out from the tiny house stepped the little chipmunk girl. She had on her sweeping cap, and her apron, and in one hand was a cloth and in the other a plate she was drying.

"Well, well, Jennie, you're as busy as ever, I see!" exclaimed Uncle Wiggily. "But are you living here?"

"Hush! No," answered Jennie Chipmunk. "I don't live here, but in this house is a dear old lady squirrel, who is so feeble that she can't get around and do all her work. So every day I come over and clean up for her, and get her meals. Oh, I just love to work!" cried Jennie.

"I believe you," spoke the rabbit. "But can't we help?"

"Of course we can," decided Kittie. "You get some wood for the fire, Uncle Wiggily, and Jennie and I will do the housework."

Then the rabbit and Kittie went in the little house, and Jennie Chipmunk introduced them to the old lady squirrel, who had to lie down in bed most of the time.

"Oh, I am very glad to see you," she said in her gentle voice. "I don't know what I would do without Jennie. She is such a help; aren't you, Jennie?"

But Jennie wasn't there to answer, for she had skipped out into the kitchen to finish the dishes, and she was singing away as she hurried along as happy as a grasshopper.

Then Uncle Wiggily brought in a lot of wood, and with Kittie to help with the sweeping and dusting, the house was soon as neat as a piece of apple pie on a Sunday morning.

"Now we must go out and gather some nuts for the old lady squirrel," said Jennie.

"What will we carry them in?" asked Kittie.

"Oh, there is a basket for you, and Uncle Wiggily can use his valise, and as for me," said Jennie, "I have little pockets in each side of my cheeks, you know." And it's really true, a chipmunk has little pouches or pockets one on each side of its face. You look the next time you see one, and notice how a chipmunk's cheeks stick out when it has a lot of nuts to carry.

So the nuts were soon gathered for the old lady squirrel, and then Jennie made a cup of tea for Uncle Wiggily and Kittie. And as they sat in the house drinking it, and talking cheerfully to the old lady squirrel, all of a sudden the fuzzy old fox came along and tried to get in. But Uncle Wiggily saw him through the window, and quickly shut and locked the door.

"Never mind," cried the fox, as he sat down outside and licked his lips. "I'll wait until you come out, Mr. Rabbit, and then I'll get you."

"Oh! what shall we do?" cried Kittie Kat in great fright.

"I'll show you," said Jennie Chipmunk. So she took the big dusting brush down off the nail, and she stuck the brush out of the window, and she waved it at the fox--waved the brush, not the window you know.

And when that fox saw the fuzzy brush waving, he thought it was the bushy tail of Old Dog Percival. And the fox was so afraid of dogs that then and there he gave three separate and distinct howls, and away he ran as fast as his legs would take him and so Uncle Wiggily and Kittie Kat could come out.

"My! But you are a smart little girl, Jennie Chipmunk," said the old gentleman rabbit. "I never would have thought of that."

Then Jennie sang her song again, and made a cherry pie for the rabbit, and he and Kittie traveled on, and the next day something else happened. I'll tell you about it right soon, when the story will be of Uncle Wiggily going berrying; that is, if the peanut man doesn't put a watermelon in the baby carriage and break the wheels so the rag doll can't eat her sawdust cake.

STORY XXX
UNCLE WIGGILY GOES BERRYING

"Well, this is a beautiful day," said Kittie Kat, as she and Uncle Wiggily walked along through the woods one morning.

"Yes, this weather is very nice," agreed the old gentleman rabbit. "I ought to find my fortune to-day. I have been traveling after it a long time, and I am getting quite tired."

Kittie Kat looked at him, and she was sorry to see that Uncle Wiggily appeared quite old. He was bending over as he walked, and he had to go very slowly, for his rheumatism was quite painful, even though he had his crutch that Nurse Jane Fuzzy-Wuzzy had made for him out of a cornstalk.

"Poor old rabbit," thought the pussy girl. "I hope that he finds his fortune soon, or it will not be of much use to him. I must look as hard as I can."

So, as they went along Kittie Kat looked under all the stones and behind the bushes and down in hollow stumps. And once, when she lifted up a stone with her claws, she saw something glittering under it.

"Oh, here is a diamond!" she cried, but it was only a piece of glass.

And, a little later Uncle Wiggily saw something shining under a big log. He cried out:

"Oh, joy! I have found some gold." But it was only a shining piece of tin. They were both much disappointed, but they kept on, still searching.

At last they came to a house that was built just on the edge of a deep, dark, dismal wood, and there was some smoke coming from the chimney of this house.

"I'm going there and ask if they know where I can find my fortune," said Uncle Wiggily.

"Better not," spoke Kittie Kat. "There may be a wolf or a fox in there. Better not."

So Uncle Wiggily looked carefully on the ground all about the little house, and then he said:

"No, Kittie Kat, a fox or a wolf can't live in here, or I could see the marks of their feet in the mud. I think a man or a woman lives in that house, and I am going to knock on the door, for they surely will be kind to us."

So, with the pussy girl following behind, Uncle Wiggily went up to the door of the little house, and knocked: "Rat-a-tat-tat!"

"Ha! Who is there?" asked a quivering-quavering voice.

"It is I--Uncle Wiggily Longears, the old gentleman rabbit, and I am looking for my fortune," he said.

Then the door suddenly opened, and there stood a little old woman, in a green dress, and she had such a long nose and such a long chin that they almost touched, and if she had been strong enough she could have cracked a nut between them.

"Oh, that's an old witch!" cried Kittie Kat.

"Nonsensicalness!" exclaimed Uncle Wiggily. "There are no such things as witches. Besides, it isn't polite to call names, Kittie Kat."

"Oh, I'm sorry," said the pussy girl, looking at her tail.

"That's all right," said the old lady kindly, and she smiled. And when she did this she wasn't at all bad looking, but instead, very nice. "Lots of people think I'm a witch," she said, "and they won't come near me. But I'm not, and I love boys and girls and animals."

"I am so old, however, that I can't go very far from home, and I would like to go off in the woods, and get some berries to make a berry pie. But alas! and alack-a-day! I cannot. But what was it you wanted, Uncle Wiggily?"

"I wanted to know if you could tell me where to find my fortune," said the rabbit.

"Yes," answered the old lady in the green dress, "I think I can tell you where to find your fortune. If you will travel on for three days more you will come to a little hill. Go up this hill, and down the other side, and there, at the bottom, you will find your fortune."

"Oh, joy!" cried the rabbit gentleman.

"How lovely!" exclaimed Kittie Kat. "Oh, how glad I am. Let's start off at once, Uncle Wiggily."

"No, not at once," said the old gentleman rabbit. "First I must do a kindness to this good old lady. I heard you say you would like some berries," he went on, "so I will go and get them."

"And I will come also," said Kittie Kat.

"It is very kind of you," spoke the old lady with the long nose and the pointed chin. So she gave them a basket in which to put the berries, and away went Uncle Wiggily and the pussy girl.

Soon they came to where there were a whole lot of bushes and they began picking the berries. The basket was almost full, and the rabbit was wondering if the lady would give him some of the berry pie after she made it, when, all of a sudden, there was a rustling in the bushes and out sprang a savage wolf.

"Ah, ha!" he growled, as he showed his sharp teeth, "now I have you both! Oh, what a good meal I will have!"

"Oh, please do not eat us!" begged the rabbit. "I am just about to find my fortune; can't you wait until after that?"

"No!" growled the wolf. Then he crouched down, ready for a spring. Uncle Wiggily and Kittie Kat were too frightened to move. They looked all around for help, but all they could see were the berry bushes. And one bush seemed redder than the others. In fact, it was as red as red ink, and, as the rabbit looked at it this bush seemed to move.

"Here I come!" cried the wolf, and he jumped up into the air. But, as he did so the very red bush seemed to leap also, and then this bush grabbed the wolf by his tail, swung him around and around and tossed him away up in the top of a tall tree.

"There! I'll teach you to play tricks on Uncle Wiggily," cried a voice, and then the red bush came over to the rabbit, and instead of being a bush it was the red monkey, and he had come along just in time to save the rabbit and the pussy. You see he looked so much like a berry bush, as he crouched down, that the wolf didn't know him, and neither did Uncle Wiggily.

"Well, this is a joyful surprise!" cried the rabbit, as he and Kittie Kat thanked the red monkey. "I'm glad to see you once more."

Then the wolf ran howling away through the woods, and the monkey helped the rabbit and the pussy girl to fill the basket with berries and they took them to the old lady, who made a pie as big as the wash basin.

And the next day the rabbit started off after the gold and diamonds. And, in case the lead pencil doesn't crawl up the white wall and make a funny picture of a man riding on an elephant, I'll tell you next about Uncle Wiggily finding his fortune.

STORY XXXI
UNCLE WIGGILY'S FORTUNE

The little old lady in the green dress, whose nose and chin nearly touched, was very glad to get the berries which Uncle Wiggily and Kittie Kat gathered. She was very sorry that the wolf had frightened them, but she thought it was just fine of the red monkey to come along when he did.

"And I just wish you could have seen him toss the wolf over the tree-tops by his tail," said the old gentleman rabbit. "It was as good as going to the circus."

"Well, for doing such a trick, the red monkey can have two pieces of my berry pie," spoke the little old woman in the green dress. And that red monkey was very, very thankful, and he ate the two pieces of pie, even down to the last drop of juice.

Of course the rabbit gentleman and Kittie Kat had some pie too, and, after they had eaten their share, and had washed their faces and paws they stayed at the house of the little old woman all night.

"For I want Uncle Wiggily to be nice and rested so he can start off after his fortune to-morrow," she said.

Well, the next morning the rabbit gentleman got ready to go. The old lady with the green dress filled his valise full of good things to eat, including some berry pie, for there were no more cherries now, you know. Then, with Kittie Kat on one side of him and the red monkey on the other side, Uncle Wiggily set off.

"Remember," called the old lady, as she said good-by, "you must travel straight on for three days, and you needn't stop on the way to look for your fortune, for you won't find it. Just keep on, and at the end of the third day you will come to a hill. Go up the hill, and down the other side, and you will then come into your fortune, and I hope you will live for a good many years to enjoy it."

"Thank you so much!" exclaimed the rabbit. "It hardly seems possible that I am going to be rich after all my travels. What kind of a fortune will it be?"

Uncle Wiggily's Fortune

"Oh, you must wait and see," said the kind little old lady.

Well, the rabbit and the pussy girl and the red monkey traveled on and on. The first day they came to a big mountain, and the monkey wanted to climb up it to see if there were any cocoanut trees growing on the top.

"No," Uncle Wiggily told him. "We must keep straight on the level road until we come to the hill." And it is a good thing they didn't climb that mountain. For on top lived a big giant who had a big club, and he might have hit the red monkey with it. Mind, I'm not saying for sure, but that might have happened, you know.

So the three friends traveled on and on, and at the second day they came to where there was a big ball of blue yarn beside a little lake. It was a nice, soft ball of yarn, such as kittens play with when grandma is knitting warm mittens for winter.

"Oh, I must stop and play with that ball of yarn," said Kittie Kat.

"No," said the rabbit, "you must not do that, for the old lady said we were to keep straight on for three days."

And it is a good thing Kittie Kat didn't roll the ball, for inside of it was a big rat, and he might have bitten the little pussy girl. Mind, I'm not saying for sure, but that might have happened.

"Now, this is the third day," spoke Uncle Wiggily when they got up one morning, after having slept in a hollow stump. "By nightfall we ought to come to the hill, and on the other side will be my fortune. Oh, how glad I am!"

So they kept on and on, stopping for dinner in a nice shady place, and toward evening they came to the hill.

"There it is!" cried the rabbit as he hurried up it. "Oh, I can hardly wait until I get to the other side."

Up he went, and up went the red monkey and up went Kittie Kat. And on the way the bad fuzzy fox sprang out from the bushes and tried to catch them, but Uncle Wiggily tickled him with his crutch and made him sneeze and fall down hill.

Then they came to the top of the hill. The sun was just setting in the clouds, and they were all colored golden and violet and purple, and oh, it was beautiful! Uncle Wiggily came to a stop. On one side was the red monkey and on the other the pussy girl. The rabbit rubbed his eyes. Then he took off his glasses and polished them on his handkerchief. Then he looked down the hill.

"Why--why!" exclaimed Uncle Wiggily. "There must be some mistake. I don't see any gold or diamonds. And this place--why, it's the very place I started away from so many weeks ago! There is where I live--there is where Sammie and Susie Littletail live-- that's the tree where Johnnie and Billie Bushytail live, and there is the pond where Alice and Lulu and Jimmie Wibblewobble, the ducks, live! This is home! There can't be a fortune here!"

Oh, how disappointed he felt. The sun sank lower behind the clouds and made them more golden and green and purple.

Then out from their homes ran the rabbit children and the squirrel brothers and the duck children, and Peetie, and Jackie Bow-Wow, and Bully the Frog, and his brother, and Dottie and Munchie Trot, and Buddy and Brighteyes Pigg--and all the others.

"Oh, here is Uncle Wiggily! Our Uncle Wiggily has come back!" they cried, leaping about in joy. "Oh, how glad we are to see you. Happy! Happy welcome! You are rich, Uncle Wiggily! Rich! Very rich!"

"Rich!" said the rabbit, rubbing his eyes and trying to stand up while all his friends gathered around him. "But I don't understand. The little old lady in the green dress said I would find my fortune here, but I don't see it."

"Let me explain," said Sammie Littletail. "Do you see that field of cabbage, Uncle Wiggily?" and the rabbit boy pointed to it.

"Yes," said the rabbit, "I see the field."

"There are seventeen million, two hundred and fifty-six thousand, nine hundred and three cabbages there," said Sammie, "and they are all yours. And do you see that field of turnips?"

"Yes," said Uncle Wiggily, as he looked down the hill, "I see them."

"There are nineteen million, four hundred and thirty-three thousand, eight hundred and sixty-six turnips," said Sammie, "and they are all yours. And do you see that field of carrots?"

"I do," said Uncle Wiggily, but he couldn't see so very far, as tears of joy were in his eyes.

"There are one hundred million, eight hundred and twenty-three thousand nine hundred and ninety-nine and a half carrots in that field," said Sammie. "Jillie Longtail, the mouse, had the half carrot because she was ill, but all the rest are yours, and you are the richest rabbit in the world--the very richest--there is your fortune. You can sell the turnips and carrots and cabbages and have forty-'leven barrels of gold."

"But--but I don't understand," said Uncle Wiggily, as he tried to hug all his friends at once.

"It was this way," said Sammie, "when you were gone we all planted things in your garden and fields for you, and we took care of them, hoeing and watering them, until they grew as never carrots or turnips or cabbages grew before. So now you have come back to us, and you are rich."

And it was true. After traveling almost around the earth in search of his fortune, Uncle Wiggily came back to find it right at home, and that's the way it often happens in this world.

Well, you can imagine how surprised he was. He hugged and kissed all his friends and then he went into his old house with Sammie and Susie Littletail, and when he had sold the cabbages and carrots and turnips for many barrels of gold, there he lived for many, many years, as happy an old gentleman rabbit as you could find in a day's journey. And though his rheumatism bothered him at times it couldn't be helped. And he gave all his friends as much money as they wanted, and they all had good times together, and lots of fun, and every once in a while Uncle Wiggily would treat everybody to strawberry ice-cream cones with cabbage or turnip sauce on.

And now I have come to the end of this book. But I still have some more stories about the old gentleman rabbit in my typewriter, in case you would like to hear them. And I am going to put them in another volume to be called "Uncle Wiggily's Automobile."

In that machine he had the most surprising adventures of which you ever heard. Why, once the doodle-oodle-um got twisted around the tinker-um-tankerum, and again the noodle-oodle-um wouldn't go, and he had to give it a drink of molasses. And again the snicker-snoozicum got the toothache. But Uncle Wiggily didn't mind, and he traveled many miles in his auto. I'll tell you all that happened, so don't worry, but go to sleep and in the morning the sun may be shining. So I'm going to say good-by for a little while, and I wish you all happy dreams.

THE END

JACKIE AND PEETIE BOW WOW

"Come on, Jackie!" called Peetie Bow Wow, the boy doggie, one morning. "Come on!"

"Where are you going?" asked Jackie of Peetie.

"Let's run off and join the circus," suggested Peetie, as he tried to stand up on the end of his tail and turn a somersault. "We can earn a lot of money."

"How?" asked Jackie, scratching his nose with his ear.

"Why, we can make money by doing tricks in the circus," went on Peetie. "We can jump over the backs of elephants, climb up to the top of the tent, and do lots of things like that. A circus is fun!"

You have read how Daddy Blake took Hal and Mab to the circus, and you will like to read about Jackie and Peetie. They are in a book called "Bedtime Stories: Jackie and Peetie Bow Wow," by Howard R. Garis, who also wrote the Daddy books.

Send to R. F. Fenno & Company, 18 East 17th Street, New York City, and they will mail the book on receipt of price, if you can not get it in your book store. The book has colored pictures.

CPSIA information can be obtained
at www.ICGtesting.com
Printed in the USA
LVHW011024280621
691317LV00005B/134